DOUGLAS ADAMS'S

STARSHIP
TITANIC

DOUGLAS ADAMS'S

STARSHIP TITANIC

A Novel by
TERRY JONES

BALLANTINE BOOKS
• New York •

Copyright © 1997 by The Digital Village and Simon and Schuster
Interactive, Inc.

All rights reserved under International and Pan-American
Copyright Conventions. Published in the United States by The
Ballantine Publishing Group, a division of Random House, Inc.,
New York, and simultaneously in Canada by Random House of
Canada Limited, Toronto.

http://www.randomhouse.com/BB/

Library of Congress Catalog Card Number: 98-96534

ISBN: 0-345-36843-6

This edition published by arrangement with Harmony Books, a
division of Crown Publishers, Inc.

Manufactured in the United States of America

First Ballantine Books Edition: November 1998

10 9 8 7 6 5 4 3 2

FOR MY DEAR ALISON

INTRODUCTION

The idea for *Starship Titanic* first surfaced in the way that a lot of ideas originate, as a mere couple of sentences out of nowhere. Years ago it was just a little digression in *Life, The Universe and Everything*. I said that the *Starship Titanic* had, shortly into its maiden voyage, undergone Spontaneous Massive Existence Failure. It's just one of those bits that you put in while you are waiting for the plot to develop. You think, "Well, I'll develop another quick plot while I'm about it." So it sat there as a couple of sentences in *L, U & E*, and after a while I thought, "Well, I think there is a little bit more to this idea," and tossed it around for a while. At one point I even considered developing it as a novel in itself and then thought, no, it sounded too much like a good idea, and I'm always wary of those.

In the mideighties I did a text-only computer adventure game version of *The Hitchhiker's Guide* with a company called Infocom. I had a lot of fun working on it. The player gets caught up in a virtual conversation with the machine. In writing such a thing you are trying to imagine and prepare for the reactions of a virtual audience. There's a lot you can do with text, to which several thousand years of human culture can attest, but it seemed to me that what the computer enabled us to do was to reach back to the days before printing and re-create the old art of interactive storytelling. They didn't call it interactive in those days, of course. They didn't know of anything that wasn't interactive, so they didn't need a special name for it. When someone stood up and recounted a story, the audience responded. And the storyteller responded right back at them. It was the coming of print that took away the interactive element and locked stories into rigid forms. It seemed to me that interactive computer-mediated storytelling might be able to combine some of the best of both forms. However, while the medium was still in its infancy, along came computer graphics and killed it off. Text may be a very rich medium, but it looks boring on the screen. It doesn't flash and hop about, and so it had to give way to things that did.

Early computer graphics, of course, were slow, crude, and ugly. As a medium it didn't interest me, so I thought I'd sit things out and wait till the graphics got good. Ten years later they were good. But interaction had largely been reduced to pointing at things and clicking. I missed the conversations that text games used to engage you in. Maybe, I thought, it would be possible to combine both . . .

At about this time, I was involved with a group of friends in the setting up of a new digital media company, The Digital Village (<http://www.tdv.com>). I began to cast around for a good subject for our first big project, a CD-ROM adventure game that would combine state-of-the-art graphics with a natural language parser that would enable the player to engage the characters in conversation. Suddenly, *Starship Titanic* stood out from the pack.

As we embarked on what grew into a huge project, the subject of novelization came up. Now, writing novels is what I normally do, and here was a peach because, in an amazing departure from my normal practice, I had developed a story which not only had a beginning but also a middle and (phenomenally enough) a recognizable end. However, the publishers insisted that the novel would have to come out at the same time as the game to enable them to sell it. (This struck me as odd since they had managed previously to sell books of mine without any attendant CD-ROM game at all, but this is publisher's logic, and publishers are, as we all know, from the planet Zog.) I couldn't do both simultaneously. I had to accept that I couldn't do the novel except at the cost of not doing what I had set out to do in the first place, which was the game. So who could possibly write the novel?

About this time, Terry Jones came into the production office. One of the characters in the game is a semi-deranged workman's parrot that had been left on board the ship, and Terry had agreed to play the voice part. In fact it was clearly the part he had been born to play. When Terry saw all the graphics and character animations we had been creating over the previous months, he became very excited about the whole project and uttered the fateful words "Is there anything else you need doing?" I said "You wanna write a novel?" and Terry said, "Yeah, all right. Provided," he said, "I can write it in the nude."

Terry is one of the most famous people in the known universe, and his bottom is only slightly less well known than his face. It has, of course, only been displayed when strictly necessary on artistic grounds, but such is the nature of his art that this has turned out to be extraordinarily often. From "Naked Man Playing Organ" and "Man in Bed with Carol Cleveland" from the *Monty Python* TV show, to "Naked Hermit in Pit" in *Monty Python's Life of Brian* (a movie that he directed naked, while the rest of the cast remained largely clothed), the creative life has been one long nudist romp for Mr. Jones. He is also renowned as a film and TV director, scriptwriter, medieval scholar, and as an author of children's books, including the award-winning *The Saga of Erik the Viking,* but none of these activities provide quite enough sheer kit removal opportunities for him. Hence his stipulation that he would write *Starship Titanic* in the nude. In comes all the freshness, lightness, and lyrical vulnerability of a man sitting at his word processor butt-naked.

I've always wanted to collaborate on something with Terry ever since I first met him almost twenty-five years ago, wearing a pretty floral dress and heaving a small tactical nuclear device on the back of a cart in a leafy suburban street in Exeter. As you are about to discover, he has written an altogether sillier, naughtier, and more wonderful novel than I would have done, and in doing so has earned himself an altogether unique credit–"Parrot and Novel by Terry Jones."

–Douglas Adams

I

"Where is Leovinus?" demanded the Gat of Blerontis, Chief Quantity Surveyor of the entire North Eastern Gas District of the planet of Blerontin. "No! I do not want another bloody fish-paste sandwich!"

He did not exactly use the word "bloody," because it did not exist in the Blerontin language. The word he used could be more literally translated as "similar in size to the left earlobe," but the meaning was much closer to "bloody." Nor did he actually use the phrase "fish-paste," since fish do not exist on Blerontin in the form in which we would understand them to be fish. But when one is translating from a language used by a civilization of which we know nothing, located as far away as the center of the Galaxy, one has to approximate.

Similarly, the Gat of Blerontis was not exactly a "Quantity Surveyor," and certainly the term "North Eastern Gas District" gives no idea at all about the magnificence and grandeur of his position. Look, perhaps I'd better start again.

———

"Where is Leovinus?" demanded the Gat of Blerontis, the Most Important and Significant Statesman on the entire planet of Blerontin. "The launch cannot proceed without him."

Several minor officials were dispatched to search for the Great Man. Meanwhile, the vast crowd simmered with mounting impatience in front of the grand Assembly Dock, where the new Starship stood veiled in its attractive pink silk sheeting. Not one member of the crowd had glimpsed even so much as a nut or bolt of the ship, but already its fame had swept the Galaxy from spiral arm to spiral arm.

Back on the launch podium, the great Leovinus had still not been sighted. A minor official was explaining yet again to the Gat of Blerontis why the "fish-paste" sandwiches were essential.

"Normally, Your Stupendous and Most Lofty Magnificence, you would be quite right in supposing that the mere launch of a starship would not be marked by such distinguished observances. But, as you are aware, this Starship is different. This Starship is the greatest, most gorgeous, most technologically advanced starship ever built–this is the Ultimate Starship–the greatest cybernautic achievement of this or any other age, and it is utterly indestructible. The Intergalactic Council therefore thought it suitable to declare it a 'fish-paste sandwich' event."

The Gat's heart sank. His last line of defense shriveled before his eyes, and he knew he was condemned to eat at least one "fish-paste" canapé before the launch was over. The taste, he knew, would endure for months. And a Blerontin month was equivalent to several lifetimes if you happened to come from Earth. Which, of course, nobody there did.

In fact, nobody in that entire throng of some fifty million Blerontinians who had turned up to see the launch of the Greatest Starship in the History of the Universe had ever even heard of Earth. And if you'd asked them they wouldn't have been able to understand you because translation blisters were not allowed to be worn at a "fish-paste" event. It was another of those stupid little traditions that made the Gat furious.*

And still Leovinus did not appear.

---

*The Blerontins insist on serving so-called "fish-paste" sandwiches during Festivals and Important Book Launches despite the fact that all Blerontins find them disgusting. It is a tradition that dates back to a time when Blerontin was an impoverished planet living on the edge of starvation. Having run out of every other kind of food, the Blerontin team were reluctantly forced to offer-up "fish-paste" sandwiches as their entry for the Centennial Intergalactic Canapés Championship. For some unaccountable reason, the "fish-paste" appealed to the jaded palates of the judges, clinched the championship for Blerontin, and paved the way for Blerontinian domination of the entire Galactic Center for aeons to come.

≡

"Everyone here is holding their breath and keeping their fingers crossed," whispered the Head Reporter of the Blerontin News Gathering Bureau into his invisible microphone. "No one has yet even caught so much as a glimpse of the fabulous Starship, but everyone is certain that it will be not only the most technologically advanced but also the most beautiful starship ever to have been created. It is, after all, the brainchild of Leovinus, to whose architectural genius we owe the great North-South bridge that now links our two polar caps, to whose musical inspiration we owe the Blerontin National Anthem 'Our Canapés Triumph Daily,' and to whose unsurpassable mastery of ballistics and biomass energetics we owe our third sun that now shines above us with its own famous on-off switch. . . . But there's news just coming in that . . . what's that? . . . Ladies and gentlemen and things, it appears that the great Leovinus has gone missing! Nobody has seen him all day. Surely they can't start the launch without him . . . but the crowd is beginning to demand some action. . . . And, uh-oh! What's that?"

A sour note had swept through the crowd as a band of short individuals, dressed in ragged overalls and flat caps, suddenly forced their way into the spectators' area. They were shouting in a language no one could understand (because of the ban on translator blisters) and they were brandishing indecipherable placards.

"It looks as if the Yassaccan delegation has managed to gain entry!" An edge of alarm had entered the Head Reporter's voice. This was mainly because he had his entire commentary written down in advance–as he always did. The thought that an unforeseen turn of events might now force him to look at what was actually going on and then improvise was a nightmare that had dogged his sleep for all the years that he had been in the reporting business.

"Um!" said the Head Reporter. He felt his head going light. "Er!" He fought for breath as he felt his bowels starting to move. "Oh! Ahm! What can I say?" He was praying that the words would come to him. In his recurring nightmare– the one that he always had after eating snork chitterlings–he was in this very situation: something unforeseen had occurred, his script was whisked away by some unseen hand, and the words just never came.

It has to be explained, in defense of the Head Reporter, that unforeseen circumstances seldom occurred during public events on Blerontin, owing to the fact that the authorities exerted a pretty tight control over these things.

"It coming yust out who!" exclaimed the Head Reporter. At that moment an unseen hand whisked away his script, and the Head Reporter felt a warm sensation all over his lower abdomen.

"I've done it! I mean! It's definitely Yassaccans! I can see them now!" That was practically two whole sentences! He *could* do it! "They've purply pinchburps! Oh damn!" It was one thing not to be able to think of anything, but how could he possibly come out with utter nonsense? That hadn't been in his nightmare. It was worse!

The truth is that this personal disaster for the Head Reporter was just one in a string of disasters that had dogged the building of the Starship. There had been rumors of corners cut: the cybernet pigeon cursors had been below-spec.; the great engine had been mislaid; Leovinus himself had quarreled with the Chairman of Star-Struct, Inc.; there had been arguments between Leovinus and his manager, Brobostigon; there had been quarrels between Brobostigon and Leovinus's accountant, Scraliontis; there had been arguments between Scraliontis and Leovinus—and so on and so on.

The fact of the matter was that the construction of the Starship had brought financial ruin on almost everybody involved, including one entire planet. Yassacca had been, hitherto, a flourishing resort of industrious folk. With the most efficient and dependable construction industry in the Central Galaxy, Yassaccans had enjoyed centuries of quiet prosperity and a high reputation. They never overcharged. They always delivered on time. They never cut corners. They were a race of proud craftsmen who had nothing to do with Intergalactic Canapés Competitions, and thus were able to devote their wealth to the well-being of their own people.

That was, until they undertook the construction of Leovinus's masterpiece—the crowning achievement of his career—the Starship that even now stands hidden from sight in its launching bay, awaiting the unveiling ceremony.

"Give us back our happy lifestyle!" shout the Yassaccan demonstrators unintelligibly to the Blerontinian onlookers.

"Planets not Starships!" roar their placards—to the baffled crowd.

"Get those bastards out of there," growls Flortin Rimanquez, the Chief of Police and Rabbits.

"Where is Leovinus?" groans the Gat of Blerontis.

2

●

Could it be only the day before that Leovinus had held his press conference? He had felt so powerfully complacent as he stepped up onto the platform. His white beard had been specially groomed by Pheronis Pheronisis, the greatest hairdresser on Blerontin, and his eyebrows had been stuck back on with a new toupee tape that was guaranteed absolutely undetectable. In many ways, this was the greatest moment in his life.

"What is it like to be not only the greatest architect the Galaxy has ever known but also the greatest sculptor, the greatest mathematical genius as well as a world-class garnisher and canapés arranger?" Exactly the kind of question Leovinus enjoyed.

There had been times, in his younger days, when he might have retorted: "Go lick someone else's arse, hack! I'm only interested in Truth and Beauty!" But somehow he found that the more wrinkles he counted on his forehead and the more problems he had with his continence and his seven-times table, the more he found a little flattery most welcome.

"I loved your Pandax Building with the interchangeable rooms and total reassembly potential!" shouted a young cub reporter with soft eyes and delightfully green lips.

"Thank you," Leovinus beamed in his most venerable and yet at the same time approachable manner.

"You look terrific!" shouted another.

Leovinus was just trying to decide which of the two cub reporters with soft eyes and delightfully green lips he should ask backstage for a little drink, or whether he should invite them both and then see how things worked out, when a male voice cut across:

"Exactly what was the scientific experiment you were working on when you had your recent accident, sir? And is it true that your eyebrows have still not grown back?" Leovinus fought off a panic attack, and told himself his eyebrows looked perfectly OK. This hard-boiled journalist was merely trying to wind him up. Then he had to fight off a panic attack about the fact that he'd just had a panic attack. "It's perfectly normal to get panic attacks at my age!" he told himself severely, while at the same time noting, thankfully, the ripple of embarrassment that had swept through the assembled media. "I'm lucky I don't have angina and a sagging bottom at my age!" Leovinus had always counted his blessings.

But something had definitely gone wrong with the press conference. A journalist, from the back, was asking a question in a tone of voice that didn't sound in the least bit ingratiating. In fact, there was something so *un*ingratiating about the voice that Leovinus could barely understand it.

"I said," repeated The Journalist in that same uncajoling voice, "how do you answer the allegations that corners have been cut on the construction of the Starship, and that there have been financial improprieties involving your manager, Antar Brobostigon, and your accountant, Droot Scraliontis?"

"Such insinuations," replied Leovinus, forming his toupeed eyebrows into the most formidable frown, and drawing his shoulders back into what he knew was his most dignified and intimidating posture, "are beneath contempt. Mr. Brobostigon is a man of unblemished reputation and has the highest regard for correct procedure. Droot Scraliontis has been my accountant for the last thirty years and has been unimpeachable throughout that time."

He could feel one of his eyebrows starting to come loose. Funny that—he always imagined that as he got older and more confident he would stop sweating whenever he had to tell a barefaced lie. But he still did.

"But isn't it true that the standard of workmanship on the Starship has dropped since the building was moved from Yassacca to Blerontin?"

"Absolute poop!" declared the Great Genius in his best how-dare-you-waste-the-time-of-a-great-genius-like-me voice (which he had been practicing recently and now had down to a tee). "I am personally checking the standards of craftsmanship on every facet of the ship, and I can guarantee that standards have—if anything—gone up since the transferral to Blerontin." He felt his other eyebrow pop loose from his forehead.

"What do you say about the collapse of the Yassaccan economy, Mr Leovinus?" It was the same dreadful journalist going on. Why couldn't someone ask him whether he preferred architecture to quantum physics or whether he felt painting should be considered a higher art form than canapé arrangement? Those were the kind of questions he was a whiz at dealing with these days. "Do you feel personally responsible at all for the present sufferings of the Yassaccan peoples?"

Leovinus went for the last-goalkeeper-at-the-net* defense: "I am an Artist, Mr. Journalist," he said in that voice of his that made grown men cringe behind their stomachs and young cub reporters with delightfully green lips feel deliciously damp all over. "Of course, I deeply regret the terrible destruction of an entire culture that their economic mismanagement has brought upon themselves, and I hereby offer my

---

*Blerontin football is played with anything up to six balls, and consequently a large number of goalkeepers is sometimes allowed.

heartfelt condolences to the people of Yassacca. I am deeply concerned that it should have been the construction of *my* vision that should have been the catalyst of their monetary downfall. But I am an Artist. My responsibility is to my Art. And I would be betraying the sacred trust of my genius were I to compromise my vision for the sake of fiscal expediency!"

"Oh! Oooooh! Ahh!" breathed one of the cub reporters, and shifted onto her other buttock.

But Leovinus scarcely noticed her. He was too preoccupied by the feeling that the entire press conference had spiralled out of control. Indeed it now seemed to be plunging toward some catastrophic conclusion that he must at all costs avoid—even if it meant forgoing a delightful drink with the delightful cub reporters who were even now gazing at him with increasingly delightful eyes and increasingly delightful green lips. In any case, he knew how any such assignation would end: he would soon find their smiles begin to grate, their soft gazes would become tiresome, probing arc lights of banality, and he would flee from the two young reporters in despair and disappointment. That was what always happened. For deep down inside him, Leovinus knew that no one was good enough for him. Why go through it all again?

Leovinus rose, unsteadily, to his feet. "Thank you," he said and was gone.

The greatest genius of his age—gone without even so much as a nod in the cub reporters' direction. It was hardly to be believed.

Despite his age, brilliance, and genius, Leovinus was not always a sensible individual. He had passions. Passions that would rise up the inside of his being and take over his magnificent brain like cholera takes over a city. And not all these passions evolved around cub reporters. At the present, his one overriding passion was the Starship. That magnificent creation. That crowning glory of his life's work.

Ever since his recent accident, Leovinus had been reluctant to go abroad; partly because his joints had stiffened up somewhat and partly because he didn't want to be seen without his eyebrows. Leovinus was not without personal vanity. He had therefore got into the habit of supervising the construction of his starship by virtual reality and telepresence—both brought to such a pitch of perfection by Blerontinian scientists that it was sometimes hard to remember which was the real thing—particularly if you were getting on a bit and your mind was on green lips and cleavages.

For that is what Leovinus's mind had been preoccupied with for many months now—but not the cleavages of young cub reporters. No. Leovinus's obsession was the cleavage of data-streams as they separated out into random thought fields; the cleavage of neuroconnectors as they bifurcated into the memory bank and the sensation retrieval system, the cleavage of separators and transjoiners linking and distinguishing those two vital processes: thought and feeling. His obsession was the heart of his Starship. He called her Titania.

Titania was the heart, the mind, the spirit, the *soul* of the ship.

A massive cyberintelligence system was required to run the ship, of course, but, as we now know, intelligence devoid of emotion is nonfunctional. However smart a robot or computer may be, it can only do exactly what you tell it to do and then stop. To keep thinking, it has to *want* to. It has to be motivated. You can't think if you can't feel. So the ship's intelligence had to be imbued with emotions, with personality. And it's name was Titania.

The Starship was Leovinus's creation. So was Titania.

It had suited Leovinus, while he concentrated on this vital heart of the ship, to work from home, but now he suddenly realized that he hadn't actually been on the ship itself for . . . well, he really didn't know how long!

Thus it was that that night, after the press conference, the Great Man put on a long snork-hair coat and made his way toward the Assembly Dock, where his masterpiece stood, awaiting tomorrow's launch.

Earlier he had received telecalls from the project manager, Antar Brobostigon, and the chief accountant, Droot Scraliontis. They had both been so full of gratitude for his defense of them during the press conference, and so reassuring about the prospects of the launch, that Leovinus found a vein in his right thigh beginning to twitch, and he kept thinking of the phrase "parrot droppings" without any viable context.

He slipped unseen down the service entrance and waited in the shadows until he saw the security robot stop to take its scheduled rest-break (as set down by Blerontin law). He then hurried across the open forecourt and disappeared into the shadow of the temporary construction workers' sheds. It was not as if he didn't have a perfect right to be there, it was just he wanted to do this without the usual fanfare and the welcoming party and the official guided tour and all the usual commotion that accompanied his public visits. He wanted to commune with his creation alone.

He looked up. There was the Assembly Dock, looming up into the night sky far, far above him. It stretched a good mile up, and the Starship—his Starship—his baby—rose up another half mile above that—ready for blastoff at midday tomorrow—precisely.s

The silk coverings flapped in the breeze that swept across the Observation Arena, over the Administration buildings, and around the Dock Structures. Leovinus felt a surge of emotion sweep through his body and engulf his magnificent brain. His heart missed several beats. His knees turned to jelly. But it was not his pride in that stupendous structure that gave him butterflies in the tummy. Nor was it the exaltation that, after all these years, it was finally complete that made him feel like a schoolboy on his first date. No, what made his hand shake as he sleeked it through his graying locks was the thought that there—in those vast halls and staterooms—Titania was waiting for him.

3

⬤

As Leovinus leaned toward the Starship, the wind picked up, blasting dead leaves, old snack wrappings, torn religious journals, pages of sentimental verse, knitting patterns, and all the other usual detritus left behind by construction workers, across the Servicing Area. The sheeting that covered the Starship flapped frantically, like the Great Ghoul in the ancient filmed entertainment *The Great Ghoul Frightens a Lot of Folk*. Leovinus shuddered with a childhood memory of fear. Then he shuddered again as he suddenly saw a figure slip from the base of the launching gantry into the shadows opposite the main steps of the Starship.

The moment he saw that figure he knew, deep in his bones, with that certainty that comes of being absolutely without any doubt whatsoever, that everything was about to go terribly, fearfully wrong.

Cautiously he edged round into the shadows where he had seen the figure disappear.

"So?" a voice spoke to him out of the darkness. It was a voice that made his stomach relocate itself around his knees—a voice that made him want to be sick—to be anywhere but where he was. Leovinus looked around for a means of escape, but it was too late. "Last-minute checkups, eh?" The figure stepped out of the shadow and confronted him. It was that dreadful journalist from the press conference.

"Haven't you tormented me enough? Haven't you already ruined a day that was meant to be one of the greatest days of my life?" That's what Leovinus wanted to say, but he merely mumbled: "Oh, it's you."

"Are you afraid something's going to go wrong with the launch?"

"Of course not!" Leovinus adopted just the right cold tone that gave nothing away. "I've merely come to pay my regards." He liked to be thought of as a bit of a sentimental-ist as well as a great brain.

"But come on! You must be a bit worried. Everyone knows that the workmanship here on Blerontin has not been a patch on the Yassaccans—in fact, you know and I know, Blerontin craftsmanship is nowhere near good enough to finish a ship of this sophistication."

"Just because the Blerontin Government chooses to employ the Amalgamated Unmarried Teenage Mothers' Construction Units there is no reason to think that the work is in any way slipshod," retorted old Leovinus. "I have every confidence in their work."

"I don't believe you," replied The Journalist.

"Very well! I'll show you!" The Great Man saw his private tête-à-tête with Titania being blown away on the wind that now buffeted them, as a small unlit work platform carried them up one of the service gantries that surrounded the great Starship.

It was only when you started getting this high up, thought The Journalist, that you really began to appreciate the full scale of the enterprise. The launch area below receded into darkness and silence as they rattled their way up the side of the vast Starship—higher and higher—until the great keel broadened out and they reached the main body of the ship. A short walk across another gantry and they were at the main doors of the spacecraft. An entry-coder read Leovinus's fingerprint and cross-checked it with a blood sample, recent hair-loss estimate, and a favorite recreational activity. The doors slid open and the two entered.

The Journalist had, of course, been in starships before, but he had never been in one like this. It was magnificent, astonishing. It was built with luxury star-travel in mind. It was built to last. It was built to impress. What's more, it was still *being* built! Two workmen were slipping into the service elevator as Leovinus and The Journalist entered the Embarkation Lobby.

"Just some last-minute adjustments," one of them mumbled to Leovinus and they were gone.

"Hm," said Leovinus in a way The Journalist freely translated as: "I wonder what those two could have been up to? They surely can't still be making adjustments this near to launch? And why didn't I know about them? I'd better check everything." It was, you understand, a very free translation.

"Donkey Databases!" exclaimed the Greatest Living Genius in the Galaxy. "Look at that!"

The Journalist looked. He saw a smartly dressed robot wearing headphones and standing on the polished marble floor of one of the most elegant rooms he had ever been in. The design was typical Late Leovinus, and yet it was imbued with a spirit that was new. It had a lightness that some critics had thought lacking in much of his earlier work, and the colors were vibrant and yet warm and welcoming. Perhaps Leovinus had at last got in touch with the feminine side of his nature—or perhaps the gentler, more approachable feel of the Starship's interior owed something to the many little finishing touches introduced by Titania.

The Journalist was at a loss to see why the Great Man was so angry, but Leovinus was already striding across to the far wall. There he yanked at a decorative panel. "Upside down!" he yelled. "I sometimes think I have to build the entire ship with my own hands!" And he produced a screwdriver and proceeded to replace the panel in the correct position. "Can't they see the entire ambient structure of the room is destroyed by exactly that sort of inattention to detail?"

The Journalist made a note in his thumb-recorder.

"Welcome to the *Starship Titanic*," the smart robot was now addressing a light-fixture that protruded from the wall. "Allow me to show you the facilities available to Second Class Travelers." The thing then turned smartly on its heels and walked straight into the nearest closed door. There was a clang and the robot fell backwards onto the highly decorative marble floor. "Here you may see the Grand Axial Canal, Second Class!" it announced proudly and extended a white-gloved hand at the ceiling.

The Journalist made another note in his thumb-recorder.

Leovinus's reaction to the robot's minor mishap was also noted down in The Journalist's thumb-recorder. It started off as "blank disbelief" and ended up as "cold fury." In between it went through a fascinating range of adjustments, all of which were noted down by The Journalist: "surprised dissatisfaction" was rapidly replaced by "stupefied indignation," which in turn quickly became "bitter resentment," which equally quickly was transformed into "burning thirst for vengeance" and on to "cold fury."

"Brobostigon!" murmured the Great Man. "That bastard has been skimping on the syntho-neurones!"

The Journalist made another note, but Leovinus turned on him so suddenly that he stuck his thumb in his mouth and pretended to be sucking at it.

"This can't happen on this ship," explained Leovinus, as he picked up the fallen robot. "Every Doorbot has a fail-safe neuron embedded in its circuitry that cancels out any nonrational activity such as we just witnessed. They are expensive items, but, I think you will agree, well worth the money."

The Journalist nodded and pretended that he had a splinter in the end of his thumb.

"Except that that BASTARD BROBOSTIGON HAS OBVIOUSLY LEFT THEM OUT! When I see him I'll . . ." But Leovinus stopped in mid-sentence.

"He's probably wondering what else is wrong with the ship," thought The Journalist with mounting excitement; he could feel a story materializing in front of him—a big story, a humongous story—and the great thing was he wouldn't have to do anything; it was all going to unfold in front of him. He knew it. And, sure enough, before The Journalist could pretend to find the nonexistent splinter, Leovinus had given the Doorbot a quick adjustment, the door had opened, and the Great Man had been bowed through into the corridor beyond.

"Enjoy your honeymoon, you lucky couple!" called the Doorbot cheerfully. The Journalist noted this down, and hurried after the great architect and shipbuilder, who had just turned right into one of the most astounding architectural spaces The Journalist had ever entered.

It was an oval space, marked out by columns. Around the perimeter wall was painted a frieze depicting the favorite recreational pastime of the Founding Fathers of Blerontin: posing for frieze-painters. Leovinus was standing staring up at a huge statue of a winged female that stood at the other end. But The Journalist's eye went down . . . down and down into what seemed like an infinity of descent, for there at his feet was the great Central Well that occupied the gigantic keel of the Starship. It was the spine of the ship, and around it, like nerve impulses, illuminated elevators constantly went up and down servicing the living quarters that were stacked below them—tier after tier. At the very bottom, far far down below, near the bilges of the ship, the Super Galactic Traveler Deluxe Suites; above them, the Second Class Executive Duplexes; and above them, far above them, the fabulously appointed First Class Staterooms.

But The Journalist scarcely had time to take all this in, for Leovinus was off, striding through the many-columned hall, toward the far vestibule—through which he disappeared.

By the time The Journalist had caught up with him, Leovinus was standing on the jetty of an even more extraordinary and beautiful feature of the *Starship Titanic:* the Grand Axial Canal, Second Class.

From the Central Well of the Starship ran two great

canals—one to the fore and one to the aft. These partly had the effect of cooling the engines, but they were also elegant recreational facilities. Up and down the canal, gondolas plied their way, the automated gondoliers all singing their own personal selection of Blerontinian folksongs—but particularly the one about the beautiful young female acrobat who fell in love with a gondolier and gave him six pnedes (approximately one million pounds sterling) as a tip.

Leovinus was doing his from-blank-disbelief-to-cold-fury routine again. The Journalist took note.

"They are not supposed to sing unless they've got passengers!" Leovinus seemed to be choking, as he clambered down into the nearest waiting gondola. The singing immediately stopped.

The Journalist joined him and said: "Perhaps they're doing a test? Reversing everything?" It was the only thing he could think of that was in any way cheery.

"Don't talk pigeon poop!" snapped Leovinus. He was clearly in no mood to be cheered. "Promenade Deck Elevator!"

"*Si!* House-Proud and Religious Mother of Twins!" said the automated gondolier. Leovinus flinched, and felt the vein twitching in his thigh.

Leovinus allowed the irritation to mount within himself, as he straightened one of the priceless No-Art Masterpieces that decorated the elevator lobby.

"Good day to you, sir, madam, or thing. And how may we assist you in your vertical transportation requirements today?" The Liftbot was half-embedded in the wall of the lift, its free hand hovered eagerly by the lever that came out of its chest.

"Just to the Promenade Deck and no backchat!" snapped Leovinus. He sometimes regretted the characters that these robots seemed to acquire, but there it was: if the ship's intelligence were to be allowed emotions—and certainly no one could doubt that Titania had strong emotions—then you had to allow her to choose robot-characters she got on with. It was no good forcing the issue. Although Leovinus had, on occasion, spoken to Titania quite forcibly about some of the characters with whom she surrounded herself. But then Titania was so tolerant, so understanding of people's failings and mistakes, that she could get on with practically anybody. He had made her like that.

The giant Promenade Deck was Leovinus's particular little favorite. Under its vast transparent canopy, passengers could stroll and marvel at the mind-erupting brilliance of the Galaxy through which they were passing. The vari-spex composition glass, of which the canopy was made, had the effect of intensifying the radiant brightness of the stars, while at the same time making it possible for the observer, by a mere twist of the head, to see—in the detail of a powerful telescope—any particular star that caught his, her, or its fancy. Around the perimeter, the pellerator (a sort of horizontal lift of Leovinus's design) enabled less-active travelers to tour the Deck without stirring an unnecessary muscle.

That was the theory. That was what Leovinus had viewed, with great complacency, on his telepresence and in his Virtual Reality Viewer at home. But that was not what he now saw in front of him. Real reality was different.

What he now saw was what is referred to architecturally as a "shambles." The vast glass canopy stretched above, as it should, displaying the immense stretches of pink silk sheeting which covered the ship. But below all was confusion. The beautiful polished parquet floor was approximately one-tenth beautiful polished parquet floor—the rest was exposed girders and cable-work, gaping holes, and protruding wires. Where the large, sprawling brasserie for Second Class Passengers should have sprawled, there was only a large, sprawling empty space littered with builders' rubble and polystyrene cups. How could this be? They didn't even use polystyrene cups on Blerontin! And yet there they were! There was no disguising the ghastly, unthinkable fact that the Promenade Deck was *not finished*—nor likely to be before the launch tomorrow morning.

The Journalist turned to see that Leovinus had fallen to his knees. He suddenly looked like the old man he was. The swagger and gallantry that usually marked his public appearances seemed to have been sucked out of him—leaving him like a crumpled empty bag.

"It can't be true . . ." he was mumbling into his beard. "Even Brobostigon . . . even Scraliontis couldn't lie so . . . I mean . . . Only this morning they told me it was all . . ."

"Good morning, sir, would you like your nasal hair cut?" A Doorbot had suddenly activated itself and was apparently trying to usher them into a cement mixer.

Leovinus cracked at last.

"BASTARDS!" He screamed at the flapping silk sheets beyond the canopy. "BASTARDS!" he yelled at the unfinished works.

Suddenly, a movement behind one of the pillars caught his eye. Taking The Journalist totally by surprise, Leovinus seemed to regain all his vitality in an instant, and had sprinted across the parquet flooring and pounced behind the pillar. A solitary worker, in drab overalls, was crouching down, trying to lose himself in a crevice of the unfinished floor.

"What the devil are you doing here?" screamed Leovinus.

The worker stood up shiftily and pretended to be adjusting a loose end of wire. "Just making good," he said.

"Making GOOD?" yelled Leovinus. "You call this GOOD?" He threw his arm out toward the vast unfinished reaches of the Promenade Deck. "We launch the ship tomorrow and there's months more work to do here!"

"Yeah . . . It's . . . bin a bit . . . slow . . ." The worker was edging toward the sleek, stainless-steel lift that offered him his only means of escape from this elderly lunatic.

"What were you doing just now?" demanded the elderly lunatic.

"Me? Just now?" replied the worker.

"Yes! I saw you doing something!"

"Me? No, I wouldn't do nothing, I only came to collect my parrot." The words fell out of his mouth and seemed to freeze in the air, and then like lumps of solid ice they hit Leovinus, one after the other, and he reeled from their impact.

"Parrot?" He said. "Parrot!!! What parrot?"

"It's ... er ... just a parrot ... you know ... couple of wings ... that sort ... you know ..."

"What is a PARROT doing on board my beautiful ship?" demanded the outraged genius.

"Oh! There's the lift!" said the worker, and the next moment he was in it with The Journalist hard on his heels; the door closed and they were both dropping to the lower floors.

"A parrot! On my Starship! What the hell has been going on?" Suddenly the great, the magnificent, the envied Leovinus was hunched up in a corner, weeping over a statue of a winged female.

"Titania!" he was sobbing. "Titania! What has happened? What shall we do?"

Titania!

The genius of Leovinus was nowhere so evident as in this, his last and best-loved creation; Titania was the brains of the ship and her statue appeared everywhere on board—serving as the eyes and ears and communicating essence of the ship's intelligence. But the ship's intelligence was also imbued with emotional life. And this is where Leovinus had excelled himself. Titania was not only the brains but also the heart of the ship.

Titania's emotional intelligence had to be carefully crafted to match her task. To run a gigantic ship of such bewildering complexity, to manage its crew, and to look after an enormous complement of passengers of different races, species, mentalities, and bodily functions and make them all feel happy, safe, and cared-for required that Titania be hugely intelligent, kind, wise, caring, serene, warm . . . and she was all these things.

Like her image—all those giant brooding angels in every room on every deck—Titania's spirit should also have been imbuing the entire ship. Quite clearly, it wasn't.

T

4

"Antar Brobostigon, please," Leovinus spat the name into the phone.

"I'm afraid Mr. Brobostigon is not here. Would you like to speak to Mrs. Brobostigon?"

Leovinus had always felt secretly sorry for the project manager's wife. He could not imagine what it must be like living with such a duplicitous, cold-blooded egomaniac as Antar Brobostigon—his pity was only slightly modified by the knowledge that Crossa Brobostigon herself was, if anything, marginally more duplicitous, cold-blooded, and egotistical. Perhaps the two canceled each other out and the Brobostigons lived a warm, intimate, and caring family life. It was a mystery to the Great Inventor.

"So nice to hear from you, Leo," said Crossa Brobostigon. Leovinus hated it when people called him that, and he knew she knew he knew she knew it. "How is the family?"

"I don't have any family, Crossa," said Leovinus with what he hoped she could hear was strained patience. "Where is Antar?"

"I think . . . in fact, I'm sure he's at the ship. He went there with Droot a couple of hours ago. Some panic about something or other—you know how those guys worry themselves sick over your ship."

He knew: about the same way an anaconda does over a goat it has just eaten.

"Is there somewhere they can reach you when they get back?"

Leovinus flicked the phone off. A deep sense of foreboding spread from his thighs, up to his abdomen and across his chest into his heart.

"Brobostigon and Scraliontis on the ship! What the devil are they up to?" The deep sense of foreboding suddenly changed into a sharp, stabbing pain in his stomach. He felt cold. He felt sick. He had to talk to the only person that could help: Titania.

He made his way down onto the canal level, along the

Grand Axial Canal, Second Class, toward the Central Dome. When he reached the vast statue of Titania that dominated the Central Dome and the head of the Central Well, he disappeared into a doorway under one of her wings. A long staircase led up to the vital heart of the ship: the secret chamber of Titania herself.

Leovinus had long enjoyed his reputation as the originator of Ironic Architecture. There was the famous house he designed for Gardis Arbledonter, the Professor of Mathematical Implausibilities at Blerontis University, in which the doors were actually radio sets and entrance and egress was gained via the bath. But here, on the Starship, he believed he had constructed one of his most satisfying constructional ironies: Titania's Secret Chamber, her central intelligence core, was located in the very middle of the great Central Dome; it formed the giant chandelier that hung above the Central Well. The secret heart of the ship was hidden in full view of every passenger and every member of the crew.

The chamber itself hung upside down, but it had been surrounded by an inverted gravity field so that, when you entered it, it appeared the right way up. The serrated ribs that transversed the Great Dome were—once you had entered the inversion field and submitted to the disorienting process of gravity reversal—in fact, long, upside-down staircases leading up to the chamber, and the Great Dome itself was a vast concave floor at the bottom of the immense Central Well that stretched up above, topsy-turvy, in an arrangement that bewildered and astonished the first-time visitor.

Leovinus sprinted up the staircase, two steps at a time. His mind focused on one thought. The love of his old age! The obsession of his aging heart! Intelligent, kind, wise, caring, serene, warm . . . Titania!

He burst into the secret chamber and gasped. His head went into a spin—and when you have a mind the size of Leovinus's, a spinning head is a formidable sensation. He vomited. He could scarcely bring himself to look at the horror before him and yet he could not take his eyes off it: Titania—his Titania—his darling creation—his joy—had been dismembered. She lay there in the center of the chamber, her hair and wings spread out in their perfect circle around her. But her beautiful, gracious head was grotesquely disfigured: her mouth had been ripped away, her eyes gouged out, and her nose torn off leaving a gaping cavity of raw microcircuitry.

But before he could even so much as mutter the word "Fiends!" Leovinus became aware of someone else in the room. A figure was crouching behind the suc-U-bus console.

"Brobostigon!" Leovinus ground the word out like a piece of gristle. "What in the name of Darkness are you playing at?" Without thinking, Leovinus found himself lunging at the project manager. A small glowing silver shard fell from Brobostigon's grasp and tinkled to the floor. Leovinus glanced down and realized that one of Titania's delicate cerebral arteries—the central intelligence core of Titania's brain—was lying against his foot. "You're destroying her!"

Brobostigon pushed Leovinus off him, and the old man staggered back and fell onto the floor across the outspread wings of his beloved creature.

"You're blind, Leovinus! You sit up there in your ivory tower, thinking you're too high-minded and pure to deal with grubby things like business and finance! Well, this whole thing's gone way out of control thanks to you!"

"What d'you mean? What are you talking about?" Leovinus was almost crying.

"This whole project is a financial catastrophe! Didn't you realize that? We're on the brink of a major fiscal meltdown!" Brobostigon was trying to get to the door, but Leovinus, with surprising agility, was back on his feet and cutting off the exit.

"So what are you trying to do?" But even as he asked the question, Leovinus suddenly saw—with total clarity—the whole plot. "The insurance!" he gasped. "You were going to scuttle my priceless ship and claim the insurance!"

"Grow up!" growled Brobostigon. "This is the real world . . ." But he never got any further. The aged genius had hurled himself upon him, hitting the manager squarely on the chin with a remarkably mundane uppercut. Brobostigon lurched backwards, caught his foot on one of Titania's wings, and fell into the suc-U-bus tray.

The moment he did, the suc-U-bus robot was activated. It leaned forward, extending its brass snout: "Always a pleasure to dispose of your rubbish!" it announced, and sucked Brobostigon up. There was an unpleasant crunching sound and a slight plop! and the project manager was gone!

The suc-U-bus system was a rather controversial part of the ship's design. In an age when telepresence was all the rage, the idea of transmitting objects around the ship quite physically and literally, by means of vacuum tubes, seemed old-fashioned and retrogressive. But Leovinus had insisted. It was yet another little irony that he cherished. He finally carried the day by using the safety argument. Physical transport was always less risky than teleportation or any pseudotravel arrangement. What's more, his suc-U-bus robots would be able to categorize and sort everything put into their tray, so if you failed to tell them where you wanted your object sent, they would do it automatically.

The system, however, was not designed for human beings, and the suc-U-bus was supposed to be programmed to reject any living human who might fall into the tray. Clearly this was yet another area where compromises had been made. Leovinus knew, with a queasy tingle, that Brobostigon had become the victim of his own plot and was now a condensed cube of detritus on its way to the ship's bilge.

The full impact of the situation began to come home to the Great Man. Here he was—the Greatest Genius the Galaxy had ever known—the day before the launch of his ultimate masterpiece, with an unfinished ship, a financial crisis (of which he had known nothing), and a dead project manager caught in the act of sabotage. This was not going to look good in the official biography.

Meanwhile, where was Scraliontis? Crossa Brobostigon had said her husband had come to the ship to meet the accountant.

Leovinus knelt beside the disfigured Titania, and lovingly slipped the silver shard into the nerve center at the base of her skull. His hand shook as he realized the other artery was also missing, in fact, now he came to look, most of her brain was missing—how had he not noticed that before? Titania's brain! So delicate it was! The slightest shock or scratch could permanently injure it.

With a ship of this sophistication it was especially dangerous to have the nerve center nonfunctional. There had been recent stories about a new phenomenon: a kind of high-tech metal fatigue that could afflict certain artifacts which had too high a density of logic systems built into them: SMEF. Spontaneous Massive Existence Failure. Leovinus knew it was theoretically possible if unlikely. He also knew that practically every molecule on the *Starship Titanic* was in some way part of the ship's logic system. If the thing were launched in its present state, who knows what catastrophe might follow?

There was no time to lose. He must retrieve all Titania's missing parts and reassemble them before the unthinkable could happen.

5

●

Some moments later Leovinus was to be found in the starboard Embarkation Lobby, yelling at the Deskbot: "Of course you know Scraliontis!" The Deskbot, while remaining perfectly polite, was showing no inclination to be helpful.

"Scrawny little man! Glasses! He's the accountant of this whole project for crying out loud!" insisted Leovinus. "You've seen him snooping about in here thousands of times!"

"Much to my regret, sir, I have been scanning my acquaintance database and am unable to come up with anyone matching the criteria you indicate. However, I am in a position to offer you a berth on the starboard Super Galactic Traveler E-Deck. The rooms are painted pink, and the noise from the disposal unit is hardly noticeable."

"I want to know where Scraliontis is!" yelled Leovinus, at the same time flashing a small gold card in front of the Deskbot. Written on the card was the legend: "Sixty Million Club."

"Certainly, sir," the Deskbot sat up brightly. "I would suggest you look for Mr. Scraliontis in the First Class Restaurant."

The First Class Restaurant was a black-tie-only affair, so the Maître d'Bot was understandably shocked when a disreputable-looking elderly man suddenly burst in and shouted: "Scraliontis! I know you're in here!"

"What an honor to have you here, sir!" exclaimed the Maître d' genially. "However, I am *sure* sir would be more comfortable in the Second Class Brasserie . . ."

"Shut up!" said Leovinus.

"Of course, sir. It will be a great pleasure to not only shut up but belt up, cease to babble, and generally get lost, for you, sir, but may I point out that we would be only too happy to oblige, sir, with some appropriate attire, if sir would be so good as to follow me . . ."

Leovinus had spotted Scraliontis, who was standing at the controls of the telepresence robot, trying to fit something into the suc-U-bus. He glanced up when he heard Leovinus's voice, smiled thinly, and hid whatever it was inside his dinner jacket.

"But sir would surely not want to feel at a disadvantage vis-à-vis the other diners, may I recommend a change of vestment before partaking of cocktails?" The Maître d'Bot blocked Leovinus's path as he headed toward Scraliontis. For a moment the Great Man lost sight of the accountant as the robot bobbed and weaved, bowing and nodding in front of him.

"Just get out of the way!" growled Leovinus.

"It would be my pleasure, sir, but may I remind you that while smoking is permitted in the First Class Restaurant it is strictly a jacket-and-tie affair, and I am afraid I shall have to call for assistance if sir proceeds any farther . . ."

"You're too late, Leovinus!" yelled Scraliontis. "This heap of junk's going nowhere! And it's going there tomorrow at noon—fast!" The accountant always did enjoy talking in elliptical sentences that didn't quite make sense; it gave him the feeling that he was in some way literary, despite his occupation.

"Stop whatever it is you're doing!" shouted Leovinus.

"We appreciate your visit, sir, and hope to see you many times in the future, but if you could just lower your voice a touch, I will show you the exit as soon as . . ."

"I said: shut up!" Leovinus suddenly turned on the robot, picked it up, and hurled it bodily at Scraliontis.

"May I recommend sir to the fire exit? I think sir will

find the plainness of the corridors more suited to his current garb . . ." remarked the Maître d'Bot as it hit the accountant full in the face, sending him sprawling. The object he had been hiding fell onto the floor with a tinkle—it was the other cerebral artery of Titania's brain! At the same moment, the robot burst apart on the elegant floor of the restaurant. Scraliontis scrambled to his feet, grabbed one of the robot's legs, and charged at Leovinus. The old man sidestepped, picked up the robot's right arm, and faced the accountant.

For a few moments the two circled each other. Then Scraliontis opened with a straight thrust into an *open line*—the robot's leg grazed against Leovinus's shoulder scoring a *high outside*. Leovinus replied with a simple *parry* from the fourth position executing a deft circle with the robot's arm that gained him the right to *riposte*. But Scraliontis was clearly fencing under a different rule book, for he went straight to a *redoublement* regardless of Leovinus's right to *riposte*. The great genius was outraged. He flung the robot's arm at Scraliontis, in an attack that certainly did not figure in any rule book, and closed in for a *corps à corps,* throwing any pretense to dueling etiquette to the wind.

Leovinus now had his hands around Scraliontis's neck. "Brobostigon!" screamed Scraliontis. "Help!"

"Brobostigon's garbage!" The normally kind and mellow face of Leovinus had taken on an evil green hue. This was mainly due to the fact that the lamp of the table on which they were now wrestling was directly under his chin.

"He may be garbage," gasped Scraliontis, "but he's got a gun!"

"He's dead!" yelled Leovinus, his fingers beginning to tighten on the accountant's neck. If he'd known Brobostigon had had a gun he would have been a bit more careful how he'd treated him.

"Arrrrgh! You're choking me!" screamed Scraliontis.

"I know! That's what I'm trying to do!" Leovinus tried to put some conviction into his voice, but he was finding it extremely difficult to make his fingers actually constrict the accountant's scrawny neck. I suppose you could say that Leovinus just did not have the killer instinct.

Scraliontis, on the other hand, did. He had tightened his hand around the table lamp—a conventionalized statuette of Titania with her wings providing the illumination. As he felt the great genius's hands falter around his neck, Scraliontis brought his knee up into Leovinus's groin. At the same time, he raised up the table lamp and brought it crashing down onto that magnificent cranium that housed Leovinus's magnificent brain.

Leovinus's hands fell from the accountant's neck; he slumped to his knees. Crack! Scraliontis brought the table lamp crashing down onto Leovinus's skull again and again. . . . The extraordinary and superb mind registered all was not right. It blocked out the pain, then realized something truly disastrous had taken place, and wisely decided to abandon contact with the outside world for the foreseeable future. Leovinus rolled over onto the restaurant floor unconscious, with blood pouring from his head.

Scraliontis stared down at him. God! He'd killed the Great Man!

In a panic, Scraliontis glanced around the First Class Restaurant. Disposing of dead bodies, although not something he'd done before, was the sort of thing his accountant's mind was really good at, and a few moments later he was hurrying out of the First Class Restaurant with a spring in his step. In his panic, however, he had forgotten the little glowing silver shard that now lay on the floor mingled with the remains of the Maître d'Bot.

Leovinus was wrapped securely in one of the great curtains that helped give the First Class Restaurant its ambience of unadulterated luxury and elegance.

6

●

While Leovinus had been thus engaged with business matters, The Journalist had been trying to pump information out of the workman who claimed to have come on board to reclaim his parrot.

"Come on!" said The Journalist. "Nobody's buying that! What are you up to?"

"I have a pet parrot," said the workman, doggedly sticking to his absurd story. "I always take it with me when I'm working. I know Mr. Leovinus wouldn't allow a bird on board, so I've been keeping it hidden. But when I came back to get it just now, I found that some bastard had opened the door of the cage and it's escaped."

The Journalist heaved his eyes heavenward. He was used to hearing cock-and-bull stories but this parrot-and-bastard one didn't even get off the slippery starting blocks of meretriciousness. "Look," he said. "I'm a journalist. I know when there's something fishy going on, and I know that you're hiding something. I'll cut a deal with you!"

The workman turned on him: "I'm really very upset! I loved that parrot."

"You tell me everything you know about the Starship and I'll not tell Star-Struct, Inc., about the parrot."

They had just reached the Central Dome area, and the worker was hurrying through the gallery surrounding the Central Well toward the port Embarkation Lobby.

"Why's the work got so behind? They've been cutting corners, haven't they? Leovinus seemed to be in the dark about it. And all these stories about the financial problems— they're true, aren't they? What's going to happen tomorrow? This ship isn't in a fit state to take off, is it?"

"That's right!" said the worker, as he strode across the Embarkation Lobby. "Everything you say is true."

"If you are enjoying your stay on board, why not celebrate with an evening in the Champion Canapé Lounge, featuring canapés from the All Blerontin Finals for six centuries?" called the Deskbot.

"So?" said The Journalist.

"So?" said the worker, turning on The Journalist and looking him in the eye for the first time. "If you see my parrot, give it this." He pressed a small metal band into The Journalist's hand and disappeared through the main doors. The Journalist looked at the piece of metal in his hand, it bore an address and a phone number, which The Journalist recognized as that of the Yassaccan embassy in Blerontis.

The Journalist spent the next half hour or so exploring the ship on his own. He discovered more unfinished areas. The starboard Embarkation Lobby, for example, was totally unfinished. Large sections of the Second Class living quarters were wanting decorating, some were even without beds. He noted everything down and returned to the Central Dome, when suddenly a figure came hurtling round the columns of the gallery and collided with him.

"Droot Scraliontis!" he exclaimed.

"I know who I am!" snapped the accountant.

"Just the man I was looking for!" smiled The Journalist.

"Argh!" Scraliontis jumped and his eyes shot guiltily over The Journalist's shoulder as if expecting to see the Homicide Police with their vicious trained rabbits pouring onto the Starship to arrest the murderer of the Greatest Genius the Galaxy Had Ever Known. "He's not dead! I swear it!"

"Who's not dead?" The Journalist couldn't believe how many juicy stories seemed to be offering themselves up to him tonight—if only he could pin one of them down. "Who isn't dead?"

Scraliontis now realized he had made a mistake. "Get out of my way!" he yelled.

"Not so fast!" exclaimed The Journalist, but Scraliontis had reached a point beyond the bounds of politeness. He shoved The Journalist back against a pillar and started to run. The Journalist picked himself up, charged after the accountant, and brought him down in what would have been referred to as a rugby tackle if they had played rugby football on Blerontin.

Scraliontis fought with the energy of a trapped animal. He scratched at The Journalist's face and punched and kicked. The two managed to stagger to their feet, still fighting like two snorks in a bucket of snork-swill (an old Blerontinian expression). The Journalist, being young and fitter, soon had the accountant backed up against the barrier rail of the Great Central Well. As he tried to restrict Scraliontis's movements, he could see past him down the dizzying depths of the Well . . . down and down seemingly forever . . . a breathtaking sight.

"Tell me what's going on!" The Journalist was pinning Scraliontis's arms to his side. "What's the scam?"

"Scam?" sneered Scraliontis. "You'll never find out!"

"Oh yes I will!" said The Journalist.

"Very well! I'll tell you everything!" replied Scraliontis

rather surprisingly. The Journalist was totally wrong-footed. He almost said: "Oh no you won't!" but he fortunately managed to stop himself.

"That's very decent of you," he managed to say, but he was not fool enough to let go of Scraliontis's arms.

"We're going to blow it up! How about that for a story?"

The Journalist was now fool enough to let go of Scraliontis's arms.

"You mean there's a bomb on board the Starship?"

"But you'll never find it!" grinned Scraliontis. "Because you won't be alive!" And suddenly Scraliontis had something in his hand. The Journalist didn't see what it was, but he felt a stab in the ribs. He staggered back, bent over, and looked up: Scraliontis was standing with one of the First Class Dining Room table lamps in his hand; the sharp, illuminated tip was dripping with blood.

At that very moment, however, there was a terrible screech and a flash of colors as a large parrot suddenly hurtled out from the arches straight at Scraliontis. The accountant tried to fend it off, but the creature's wings kept beating at his face and its beak was tearing at his nose, and the accountant scrambled back against the barrier rail, flailing with his arms and screaming, "Get it off! Get it off!"

And then it happened.

It was one of those ironic moments that fitted perfectly into Leovinus's current architectural style, and it gave The Journalist his first piece of hard evidence that corners had indeed been cut during the construction of the *Starship Titanic*.

Scraliontis had, of course, been the main instigator of the plan to reduce the construction costs of the Starship. It had become clear that the whole project could never break even, let alone go into profit. It was, in fact, heading for total enormous financial disaster. His and Brobostigon's reputations and personal fortunes were both on the line. There was only one clean, simple, rational solution—and that was to scuttle the ship and claim the insurance.

The ship was, of course, already heavily insured, but Scraliontis made sure that those policies were beefed up and that all moneys repayable were routed through companies owned by himself and Brobostigon. Construction costs had to be cut to the bone, and building restricted to the merely cosmetic. He had, unbeknownst to Leovinus, instructed contractors to halve and then quarter the specifications of any number of elements on board.

One of the materials that had been generously economized on was the metal employed in the barrier rail surrounding the Great Central Well. "After all," Scraliontis had remarked, "there aren't going to be any passengers to lean on it, so why make it unnecessarily strong?"

The reason, he now realized, was that it might not be a *passenger* who leaned on it; it might actually be the project accountant who leaned back against it, in a moment of forgetfulness while under assault from a parrot. But the realization came too late. Scraliontis heard the feeble metal crack and next moment found himself falling backwards into the abyss.

By the time the horrified Journalist had made it to the broken rail and looked down, Scraliontis was a tiny figure–still no more than a third down the Great Central Well–turning gently in circles, waving his arms and shouting up ever more faintly: "Bloody parrots!"

The parrot in question alighted on The Journalist's shoulder.

"Bloody accountants!" it said.

1

•

The vicious rabbits had been brought back under control. The overexcited riot police had been calmed down by their chief, and the Yassaccan protesters lay groaning in mangled bloody heaps on the ground. It had been a totally successful exercise in crowd management. Flortin Rimanquez saluted smartly as he reported back to the Gat of Blerontis.

"Everything under control, Your Magnificent Beneficence," he said. "You may proceed with the launch."

"But Leovinus is still missing," replied the

Gat, who was extremely concerned that he might miss out on the great photo opportunity of being seen arm in arm with the Greatest Genius the Galaxy Had Ever Produced. It was exactly the sort of thing his sagging poll ratings needed, his publicity agent had said. "Whatever you do, get your photo taken next to Leovinus." It was, indeed, the single most important thing on the Gat's mind throughout the whole proceedings.

"With regret, Your Ultimate Lordship," said the Chief of Police with another sharp salute. "The crowd down there is fifty million. They are getting extremely restive. I humbly suggest that we get this launch over and done with so my boys can start dispersing them at once—otherwise we might all be sorry."

The Gat could see what he meant. The crowd had already closed in over the bodies of the unfortunate Yassaccan demonstrators, and he could see fights breaking out all over the launch area.

"Very well," he sighed. "No, thank you!" he added, as the minor official offered him a "fish-paste" sandwich.

"I'm afraid you have to, Your Magnificence, it's all part of the ceremony!" whispered the minor official hurriedly.

The Gat groaned. The band struck up the Blerontin National Anthem and the crowd all stood on their heads—as they always did as a mark of respect to the monarchy.

"Sirs, madams, and things," intoned the Gat of Blerontis

into the ceremonial microphone. "This 'fish-paste' sandwich is delicious!"

A cheer went up from the crowd. The Gat sighed again, it was such a pathetic ceremony, he thought. "And now it is my privilege to launch this—the greatest starship ever built! Fellow Blerontinians, this is a proud moment for all of us. I name this Starship . . . *Titanic* . . . May luck be with all who fly with her."

And so saying, the Gat let swing the beribboned bottle of French champagne* so that it smashed into the bow of the ship. At the same moment, the minor official pulled a cord, and the sheeting that hitherto had covered the great Starship fell to the ground in a gentle cascade of pink silk.

There was a gasp from the multitude. Even a people used to the sight of great starships had never before witnessed one of such vast structure, such flawless design.

"Isn't she beautiful?" sighed countless male starship spotters, scanning their binoscopes over the hull for the registration number.

"Your mummy built that . . ." murmured countless unmarried teenage mothers to their infants.

"It's a triumph!" exclaimed the Head Reporter, suddenly

---

*It may seem odd that a civilization that had never even heard of the planet Earth and certainly had no idea of its existence should use French champagne for such an occasion. The explanation is rather complicated and involves a lot of stuff about time warps and black holes and an Intergalactic Smuggling Ring. If I were you I simply wouldn't worry about it and just get on with the story.

remembering what his script had had written down for this moment.

There was a ghostly roar, as if of seas beating on a distant shore that lies beyond the horizon of thought, as hugely, magnificently, the fabulous ship eased its way forward from its construction dock. It then picked up speed, swayed a bit, wobbled a bit, veered wildly, and, just as the crowd was about to scream out in disbelieving terror, it vanished. Just like that. It had undergone what was about to become famous as SMEF (Spontaneous Massive Existence Failure).

In just ten seconds, the whole, stupendous enterprise was over.

8

"We're going to put the bathroom here and the door over there," said Dan.

"It's terrific," said Nettie. "But . . ."

"I thought the bathroom was going to be there and the door was going to be over here?" said Lucy.

Why did he always get it so wrong? Dan always made the effort and yet, no matter how hard he tried, the things he and Lucy had discussed only the day before entirely eluded him or came out all garbled.

"That's what I meant," said Dan.

"It's terrific," said Nettie. "But, I have to tell you something . . ."

She was interrupted by Nigel, who was sniffing around the cellar. "You can smell the centuries of vinous pleasure oozing from the very brickwork!" he shouted up.

"The place is only a hundred and fifty years old!" Lucy shouted back down.

"It was built as a rectory," Dan murmured to Nettie.

"Mmm, terrific," said Nettie. "But, look, Dan . . ."

"You're not kidding!" Dan felt the enthusiasm welling up from deep inside him the way it always did when he needed it to. "We're going to have the restaurant here, on the right as you come in—not your nouvelle cuisine but state-of-the-art Californian. And here there'll be a bar."

Lucy gave him a withering look, but mercifully she didn't correct him. Oh, yes, now he remembered, the restaurant was going to be on the left; it had started off on the right, then they'd changed it to the left, then they'd changed it back to the right again, but then Lucy had pointed out that the kitchen would be better on the other side so they'd gone back to the left. How the hell was he supposed to remember anyway?

"Terrific," said Nettie. "But look . . ." Her voice trailed off as Nigel reappeared. Nettie looked stunning in her simple Gap T-shirt that didn't quite cover her midriff and hand-knitted waistcoat. Nigel put his arm round her.

"Like what you see?" he asked.

"Mmmm," said Dan.

"I mean the house," said Nigel. Dan couldn't stand that effortless, slimy superiority that his business partner could turn on and off like a hose pipe of cold water. No wait a minute! Make that *ex*-business partner. The Top Ten Travel Company was no more. They had just sold it for what seemed to Dan a ridiculously satisfactory amount of money.

"It's just what Lucy and I have always dreamed of, isn't it, Buttercup?" he said. Lucy hated it when he called her pet names in public, but she had never told him, so she blamed herself. She could see he thought she liked it, and this minor deception had now been going on for so long that she couldn't see how she could possibly correct it. How long had they been together? It must be all of thirteen years—in fact, since the very early days of the Top Ten Travel Company when Nigel had chatted her up in a bar on Santa Monica and introduced her to his business partner.

Lucy had originally been strongly attracted by the suave Englishman, but as they'd all got to know each other she found Dan, the quiet East Coast University man, more real and more understandable. In fact, the more they got to know each other, the more she wondered why on Earth nobody could see at first glance what a complete sleazeball Nigel was.

"We're going to call it The Watergate Hotel," said Dan.

"Won't that put off Republicans who still want to bug each other?" asked Nettie.

Nigel patted her bottom. "Go and turn the car around, there's a good girl," he said. And Nettie trotted off on her high heels down the steps of the elegant early Victorian rectory, into the night.

How can she let him treat her like that? thought Lucy to herself, but said: "When are you going to sign the final release forms for the company, Dan?"

"Oh, er . . . I'm not sure . . ." Dan seemed suddenly nervous. "I don't think Nigel's got them yet. . . ."

"The forms should be waiting for us back at the hotel," said Nigel before Lucy could explode. Exploding was a reaction to Nigel which she found increasingly natural. However, in this case, the fuse was lit, and would keep burning until they got back to the hotel and found that (surprise! surprise!) the release forms hadn't arrived after all and that that damned delivery company had let Nigel down yet *again*. Poor Nigel! He always had some excuse or other.

They turned the lights off in the empty house and made their way across the drive in the darkness. Above them, the stars filled the cold night sky with astonishing clarity.

"Why hasn't Nettie turned the car round?" A twitch of irritation gave Nigel's suavity a razor's edge.

When they got to the car, they found Nettie squinting through the lens of a single-reflex Minolta that she had placed on its roof.

"What on Earth d'you think you're doing, Bozo?" When Nigel sounded playful he was always at his most dangerous.

"Sh!" said Nettie. "I'm taking a photo of the house. Don't jog the car."

"I don't know whether you've noticed, Einstein." There was sheer joy in Nigel's voice. He loved ridiculing his girl-friends. "But it's night."

"'Sright!" replied Nettie, not moving her blond head so much as a millimeter. "I'm taking a photo called: 'Dan and Lucy's Hotel Beneath the Stars.' Maybe you'll frame it and hang it in the entrance hall?"

"You can't take photos at night unless you've got a flash, Dumbbell." Nigel opened the car door.

"Hey! You've jogged it!" Nettie screamed out.

"Get in, Brainbox, I'll drive," said Nigel.

"I guess it was long enough," said Nettie to Dan.

"Terrific," said Dan.

They were all just about to get in the car when a sudden wind swept across the vicarage lawn and the trees blew almost as if a hurricane had hit them—except that they blew in all directions.

"Jesus!" exclaimed Dan, gripping the side of the car. "What was that?"

"Look!" breathed Lucy. She was pointing up in the sky. "A falling star!"

"Make a wish!" shouted Nettie.

"Holy moly!" growled Nigel, who was the sort of person who had always preferred Captain Marvel to Superman. "Will you look at that?!"

Above them, a most extraordinary thing was happening.

A ring of cloud had suddenly formed immediately overhead and then spread out—like a nuclear explosion—until the entire sky was covered by a broiling layer of evil-looking cumulus. Nigel went weak at the knees; Lucy shuddered; Dan felt his stomach jump; and Nettie simply gaped.

But there was more to come.

The four Earth folk heard a ghostly roar, as if of seas beating on a distant shore that lies beyond the horizon of thought, and then hugely, magnificently, and without warning a vast metallic prong descended from the cloud and sliced their elegant former Victorian rectory (with planning permission for commercial development) in two.

Nigel gaped; Lucy gaped; Dan gaped.

"Terrific!" murmured Nettie.

There was no other noise save the wind rushing crazily around in the trees, as if it were looking for a place to hide, and the occasional thud of falling masonry, as bits of the rectory that had not already been dislodged by the impact crashed to the ground.

The thing itself was shiny and vertical and it stretched up into the clouds as if it always had. It was so huge—so present—that it seemed to have a perfect right to be there. As they watched, a small pinpoint of light descended down the side and disappeared into the ruined house.

The swirling clouds, meanwhile, had begun to disperse, and by the time the pinpoint of light started to descend for the second time, the clouds had cleared to reveal the full, awesome vastness of the thing. The wide blade or prong that had buried itself in the house stretched up and up almost a mile into the sky, and there it seemed to widen out into an immense metallic body—rather like a gigantic submarine.

"It's a spaceship," murmured Nettie, and she began to walk toward it as if mesmerized, her camera dangling forgotten from her wrist. Suddenly, the pinpoint of light shot up again.

"Don't! Nettie! Come back!" Dan yelled.

But Lucy was already racing after Nettie. So Dan raced after Lucy. Nigel, in the meantime, tried his best to help by hiding under the steering wheel.

"Don't go near it!" said Dan.

"Nettie!" Lucy was pulling her arm trying to head her back to the car. "We . . . we . . . don't know what it is!"

"It's wonderful . . ." murmured Nettie. Something in Nettie's tone made all three of them look up at the great thing and stop whatever it was they were doing. Confronted by something so immense, so beyond their experience or imagination, anything they did suddenly seemed irrelevant, pointless.

The pinpoint of light had descended into the house for a second time, and there was a glow coming from the hallway. As the three of them brought their eyes back down to Earth, they froze: a shadow had appeared on the window of the front door.

"There's something coming!" Dan could feel his knees

beginning to quiver. Lucy pulled at Nettie's arm. But Nettie edged forward—as if eager to greet whatever it was that was even now opening the front door of the destroyed vicarage . . .

"Aggggh!" screamed Lucy as the thing emerged into the starlight.

"Good evening to you, unknown life-forms," said the thing. "The proprietors of Starlight Travel, Inc., would like to apologize for any inconvenience you may have suffered due to the inadvertent emergency parking of their vehicle."

"Arrrrrghhh! Aaaaaaarggghhh!" Lucy was by now screaming incredibly well. Nigel was covering his ears and trying to get even farther under the steering wheel of the car.

"It's all right, Lucy!" Dan was trying to calm her down.

"Arrrrghhh! Aaaaaagghhhh! Arrrrrgggghhhhh!" Lucy was not about to be calmed down by anybody. She was confronted by an Alien from Outer Space, and she was jolly well going to have a good scream.

"Sh!" said Nettie. "It's talking to us!"

"Quite," said the Thing from Outer Space. "By way of apology, may we have the pleasure of offering you a free cruise aboard our Starship?"

"Perhaps another day . . ." said Dan.

"Aaaaaaaarrrrgggh! Arrrgh! Aaaaah! Aaaggghhhh!" continued Lucy.

"Yes!" cried Nettie. "I'd love to!"

"Come with me, madam," said the Thing from Outer Space, and it turned smartly back into the ruined house.

"Well? Come on!" said Nettie. "What a hoot!" And before either Lucy or Dan could stop her, she had followed it through the front door.

Dan hesitated, and then realized he had no choice; before Lucy could start screaming again, he was racing after Nettie, and Lucy found herself racing after Dan.

The Thing was standing by an illuminated porch, and they could now see that it appeared to be nothing more frightening than a smartly dressed robot wearing headphones, who bowed politely to them and apologized for having to invite them into the service elevator.

"Please do not be alarmed," it said in a soothing voice. "I can assure you that the *Starship Titanic* is the most luxurious and technologically advanced Intergalactic Starship ever built."

It bowed again and ushered them in, and somehow or other—neither Dan nor Lucy nor Nettie could later quite explain why—they all three found themselves entering the elevator. Before they knew what was happening, the steps had retracted up behind them and the robot had flicked a switch.

"I apologize once again for having to bring you in by the service elevator," remarked the robot, "entrance to the Starship is normally at Embarkation Level."

"Hey!" exclaimed Dan. "How come you speak English?" Dan felt better now that he'd found something concrete to question.

"I beg your pardon, but I am not speaking . . . what did you say—'English'? All robotic functions on this ship are equipped with infraviolet translation sensors which automatically scan the brain impulses of passengers for language patterns. These patterns are then rearranged inside your heads so that you can understand and speak intelligibly while on the ship. You are actually speaking and understanding Blerontinian. Pretty convenient for writers of science fiction, huh?"

Dan wasn't sure what to make of this last remark—was the robot inferring that he was nothing more than a figment of some writer's mind and that this whole thing was not really happening? However, before he could think any further along these lines, his mind was overwhelmed by the fantastic situation in which they now found themselves: they were speeding vertically up the vast keel toward the main body of the Starship, a mile above the surface of the Earth.

Nigel stabbed out a number on his mobile, and called half-heartedly out of the car window: "Dan? Lucy? Nettie?" But his voice barely reached the crumbled brickwork of the ruined house.

The next moment he heard a ghostly roar, like seas beating on a far-off shore.

"Hello?" said his mobile. "Oxford Police Station. Can I help you?"

Nigel didn't reply. He was too busy watching the vast

unbelievable thing as it rose up into the air again and disappeared toward the Milky Way.

"Hello? This is Oxford Police Station," insisted his mobile phone. "Who is this?"

Nigel looked at the smashed Victorian vicarage, and the driveway where his friends had stood a few moments ago, and replaced his mobile on its cradle. "It didn't happen," he murmured to himself. "It didn't happen."

You might have thought there was a tinge of relief in the way his shoulders relaxed, but of course you would have dismissed such an idea as total fantasy.

In any case, at that same moment, Nigel suddenly became very unrelaxed indeed. In fact, he very nearly jumped out of his Armani trousers; he certainly hit his head on the roof of the car.

"Ouch!" he yelled.

An old man with a flowing white beard was sitting quietly in the passenger seat; there were tears in his eyes and one of his eyebrows was just about to fall off.

9

The moment the ship took off, Dan felt a sinking feeling in his stomach. This was, of course, simply the result of the incredible g force that was being exerted upon his body. But Dan, who had no idea that the ship *had* taken off, merely thought he was getting nervous. The sinking feeling in the stomach was quickly followed by a draining of blood from the brain, leading to momentary light-headedness, followed by total blackout.

If he hadn't just passed out, Dan would have noticed that the takeoff had affected Lucy and Nettie in an identical way—even though none of them knew what was happening.

"Nothing to be alarmed about, sir, madam, and thing," the polite robot seemed to be addressing this last at the now comatose Nettie. "A perfectly routine takeoff. You life-forms have a good snooze while us machines get on with running the ship." The Doorbot, itself, then blacked-out and lay in a tidy heap, while the ship accelerated at speeds far beyond its original specifications, toward an unknown quarter of the Intergalactic Space-Time Continuum.

The robots on board must have recovered consciousness before the human beings. Nettie found herself undressed and tucked up in bed in a tiny cabin about the size of her flat back in Haringay.

Apart from the size, everything about the place was unfamiliar. The sheets on the bed were made of some material that felt like silk but much thicker and heavier. The mug holding the toothbrush bore a picture of an elderly Egyptian opera singer—or at least that's who it looked like to Nettie. She'd once received a post-card of an elderly Egyptian opera singer—and had kept it in a drawer. The toothbrush itself was rather weird, since it kept ducking its head and brushing its own handle, rather like a bird preening itself.

Opposite the bed was a television on which a snowstorm seemed to be the only entertainment. Nettie picked up the remote, aimed it at the TV, and started pressing buttons.

A cocktail cabinet rose out of the floor; a Dustbot scuttled out of the clothes cupboard, picked up an invisible speck of dust, squeaked "Thank you for appreciating a clean environment!" and hurried back out of sight again; the door opened; the lights went on and off but the TV resolutely refused to show any program other than the snowstorm.

"Ah! Hi! I'm glad to see you have found your Personal Electronic Thingie, please keep it with you at all times since it is your communication with the *Starship Titanic*. Welcome aboard." Nettie found herself apparently being addressed by the standard lamp that stood in the corner of the cabin. She instinctively pulled the sheets up to cover her breasts.

"Wowee! I don't blame you keeping those babies to yourself!"

"Will you turn around while I get dressed!" said Nettie. The lamp turned around obediently. It was the same on the other side. "Will you please go away?" she said.

"Hey! That'd be groovy! I've had it up to here with standing around in this cabin anyway!" The standard lamp walked smartly toward the door. "Oh, by the way," it said breezily. "I'm your Bellbot. Anything you want, just ask me. I'll be standing outside. Wow! It's great to get a change of scenery!" And it closed the door.

"I'm sure that robot's not meant to behave like that," said Nettie to herself, as she threw on her clothes and examined the thing she had mistaken for the TV remote control. On it were a variety of buttons. One of them bore an icon of the Bellbot so she pressed it and the door reopened and the Bellbot peered in.

"Wowzeee! You look terrific in that Gap T-shirt!" it exclaimed.

"Will you please refrain from making personal comments!" said Nettie rather crossly.

"Hey! No offense, man!" The Bellbot seemed genuinely hurt. "What can I do for you?"

"First, I want to meet up with my colleagues. Second, I think we probably would like to know how to get off this ship."

"Hot dog!" the Bellbot snapped its fingers with a metallic ping. "You mean there are more hot little numbers like you around?"

"You are behaving most impolitely for an android!" Nettie knew how to address a robot. "Would you please keep your personal comments to yourself or otherwise I will have you reported—and you know what that'll mean."

The Bellbot froze to the spot. "Hey, man! I'm a genuine 'personality transfer' bot. It's my character!"

"Well I don't like it. And you're here to serve me so just stop it at once."

The robot went all sulky. "All right! Don't go on about it."

"Do you know where my friends are?"

"Adjoining rooms?" suggested the Bellbot.

Nettie was out of her cabin in a moment. Every door along the narrow corridor, that curved around out of sight, had writing on it.

"What does this say?" she asked. By way of answer the robot produced a pair of spectacles and offered them to Nettie. Nettie hesitated, then put them on.

"Translatorspecs," explained the Bellbot unhappily.

Nettie could now see that every door had a name: "Hyacinth," "Jasmine," "Delphinium," and so on.

"How tacky," murmured Nettie, and she started knocking on "Cauliflower." After a dozen or so vain attempts on various flora, she turned on the Bellbot, which was walking quietly behind her with its hands folded behind its back. "Look! Do you or do you not know where my friends are."

"I do not," said the robot.

"Do you or do you not know how I can go about finding them?" Nettie was phrasing her questions carefully.

"I do," said the Bellbot after some thought.

"Then tell me how," said Nettie.

"Guest list," announced the robot.

"And where is that?"

"Deskbot–Embarkation Lobby–Embarkation Floor," replied the bot.

"Can't I just ring from my room?"

"Not from the Super Galactic Traveler Class Suites, no."

"Then show me the way to the Embarkation Lobby," said Nettie.

"Ah!" replied the Bellbot, "I'm afraid I can't leave this deck, but if you go along to the lifts, the Liftbot will take care of all your vertical transportation requirements, and then a Doorbot will escort you round the Embarkation Lobby."

Nettie sighed. She could already tell that traveling Super Galactic Class was not going to be glamorous.

Lucy came to her senses to hear a loud knocking sound. She sat up and looked around an unfamiliar room. It was tiny, cramped, and had a hideous lampstand in one corner. The television wasn't working properly and the color scheme was a ghastly pink. There was a constant grinding sound coming from underneath the floor and besides that there was this wretched knocking on what she now began to recognize as the door.

"Lucy!" Lucy now realized there was a voice accompanying the knocking. "Open the door!" It was Dan.

"How?"

"You've got a little remote control thingie—use that," shouted Dan.

After a bit of fumbling she managed to get the door opened, and there was Dan, standing in a dingy corridor running his fingers through his hair like he always did.

"Thank God you're OK!" He smiled that mile-wide of his, and Lucy flung herself at him as if she were drowning.

"What happened?" she cried.

"We're going to find out." Thank goodness he sounded more confident than he must have felt.

"We're in that spaceship, aren't we?" Lucy wished she didn't sound so unconfident, because now that she had Dan there, she really felt everything was going to be all right.

"Let's find Nettie and get out of this thing as fast as possible," said Dan. "Apparently we can only locate other passengers by going up to the Embarkation Lobby. You'd think a thing this sophisticated would have room-to-room telephones!"

The lift entrance in the Super Galactic Traveler Class offered no view of the Central Well. But once you stepped into the lift, the sudden sheer vastness of the Well took you by surprise. Lucy and Dan found themselves speechless.

"Huh!" said the Liftbot. "If sir, madam, or thing would care to give some indication of their vertical traveling requirements I might be able to get on with my job, such as it is."

"The Embarkation Lobby, please," said Dan.

"You're asking *me* to go *up*?"

"Am I?" asked Dan.

"The Embarkation Lobby is on the Embarkation Level, sir," said the Liftbot in the tone of voice most people would only dream of using to address particularly stupid patches of damp.

"Then that's where we'd like to go."

"*Up?*"

"I suppose so."

The Liftbot fetched-up a groan from deep within, and

muttered to itself: "Young people nowadays! Don't give a tinker's cuss for them as went through the hell of two world wars that left some of us with one arm and a broken marriage."

Lucy kicked Dan, as she felt him about to reply. "Just take us to the Embarkation Lobby," she said in her best Rodeo-Drive-No-Hostages-Taken voice, which she used when buying antique rugs.

The Liftbot stifled a pathetic sniffle, put its hand to the handle sticking out from its chest, and pushed it up with a sigh. The elevator gathered speed and the humans were once again silenced by the spectacular magnificence of the Starship.

Lucy put her hand into Dan's. In her dreams she had imagined places of such scale and splendor, but she had always known that they belonged strictly to the world of the imagination. And yet here she was—in an interior that matched up to her dreams. The old rectory, which Dan had been so crazy about, looked pretty tawdry compared with this.

She glanced sideways at Dan. She couldn't guess what he was thinking. Then again, she never could.

As they stepped out of the elevator into the loggia at the top of the Great Central Well, they caught sight of a blond figure in high heels disappearing into the far door. By the time they reached the Embarkation Lobby, they found Nettie apparently deep in conversation with a desk light.

"This is the Embarkation Lobby, sir and madam." A Doorbot had already wheeled over and was gesticulating in front of them in a rather meaningless fashion. "As Super Galactic Travelers you are entitled to pass through this lobby but you may not use the seating accommodation or the bathrooms. Super Galactic Traveler Class facilities are available on your own decks."

"Look, we're not traveling," said Dan. "We just want to know how to get out of this thing."

At that moment Nettie, who seemed to be getting nowhere with the desk light, spotted them. "Hey! There you are!" she called, and then turned back to the desk light and said: "Listen, bulb-brain, you can fill your own request forms in—in triplicate—and shove them up your lampshade!" The desk light rested its head in its hands and pretended to be looking somewhere else.

"Get off this thing?" the Doorbot was repeating to itself, as Nettie joined them.

"Yeah!" replied Dan. "We want to get out—like the quickest way."

"Ohh!" Nettie looked a bit puzzled. "Don't you just want to look around a bit?"

Dan found he was more and more surprised by this extraordinary woman. "Look around a bit?" he exclaimed. "Aren't you scared?"

"Well, a bit—but it's so *exciting*! And these things seem to be perfectly harmless." Nettie gave the Doorbot a chuck under the chin. It sniffed and pretended to flick a bit of fluff off its sleeve. A Dustbot shot out from the skirting, picked up the imaginary bit of fluff, squeaked, and shot back into the skirting again.

"It's amazing, isn't it?" ventured Lucy uncertainly.

"Sensational!" agreed Nettie.

"But we've got to be sensible," said Dan, adopting his "I'm in charge" manner that never fooled anyone. "We ought to find the exit—so we know where we are—and then, maybe, we could explore a bit if you really want."

"I'm afraid you can't, sir." The Doorbot sniffed in that particular way designed to make anyone who hasn't paid a fortune for their ticket to snooty travel agents in Kensington feel like unwanted dandruff.

"Can't what?" said Lucy.

"I am afraid you can't leave the ship," replied the Doorbot. "Now, if you wouldn't mind hurrying through to your own decks . . ."

"Wait a minute!" Dan had decided to turn nasty, which, in his case, was usually as nasty as a packet of Band-Aids. "What do you mean 'we can't leave the ship'?"

"Are we *prisoners*?" Nettie sounded faintly thrilled.

"No, madam or thing, of course you are not prisoners; it is simply a physical impossibility for you to leave at this moment in time because the Starship is in flight." The Door-bot coughed and indicated the loggia and the Great Central Well. "I suggest you all go down to the Super Galactic

Traveler Class Restaurant where you will encounter plain home cooking with a great doorway."

The news that they were in flight had a remarkable effect on the three human beings. If there had been a window, they would all have undoubtedly dashed to it. As there was not, all the energy that would have gone into that dashing had to be used up somehow. Nettie used it up by doing some aerobic movements designed to release stress. Lucy and Dan used it up by shouting at Nettie.

"You see what you've done! Oh my God! We're in space! It's all your fault!" Dan chose plain abuse.

"I knew it!" Lucy was going for guilt-provoking self-recrimination. "I knew we shouldn't have followed that dumb peroxide airhead!"

"Please refrain from shouting on the Embarkation Level. There may be First or Second Class passengers about. You may shout as much as you want on the Super Galactic Traveler Class decks," and again the Doorbot indicated the way down.

Nettie was holding up her hands. "Hey! Hey! Guys! Calm down!"

"Why should we calm down!?" Dan had hit Histrionic Mode. "You've just destroyed our future home! You've forced us onto an alien spacecraft! And now we're not even on Earth anymore! God knows how we'll ever get back!"

"Please!" said Nettie. "I didn't destroy your future home . . ."

"No! No! I know! I'm sorry! I just got carried away!" Dan didn't know why he'd said that.

"And if we really are in the situation this robot tells us we're in, we'd better keep our heads and decide how to get out of it."

"Arrrgggggghh! Aggggggghhhhhh! Arrrrghhhhhhhhhh!!" Lucy had decided to set aside her admiration for the fabulous decor of the ship and had reverted to Primal Scream Mode.

"Please scream on the Super Galactic Traveler Class decks only!" urged the Doorbot.

"DO?!" shouted Dan. "DO?! WHAT *CAN* WE DO?!"

"I suggest," said Nettie firmly, "we find the Captain—there must be one—explain our situation, and ask him to take us home."

"Fine! Oh, fine!" Dan was beside himself with sarcasm. "FINE! Find the Captain! Why didn't I think of that? Oh, yes! Brilliant idea! . . . Actually, that *is* a pretty good idea."

"Arrgh! Aaaaaagh! Arrrrrgh!" continued Lucy after a short pause.

"Shut up!" said Dan. It was the first time he had ever spoken to Lucy like that, and she shut up in surprise.

"Where can we find the Captain?" Nettie turned to the Doorbot, who was looking about anxiously to make sure no other passengers were being incommoded by all this Super Galactic Traveler Class screaming.

"The Captain, madam or thing, is to be found on the Captain's Bridge," said the Doorbot coldly with killing logic.

"And where do we find that?"

"You don't," said the robot firmly. "The Captain's Bridge is accessible only from the First Class accommodation."

"Well, surely we can just go through in order to get to the Bridge," reasoned Nettie.

"I'm afraid not," sniffed the Doorbot. "All traveling area restrictions are strictly observed on this vessel."

"Oh come off it!" exclaimed Dan. "This is an emergency!"

"Over there!" said Nettie. She had just put on her translatorspecs and could now read the sign—FIRST CLASS PASSENGERS ONLY BEYOND THIS POINT—on a door at the other end of the lobby.

"That's pretty neat!" exclaimed Dan, when Nettie had explained how she knew which way to go.

"Arrrrgh!" said Lucy. "Sorry! I didn't mean to scream! It's just that robot moved so fast!" And it was true: the moment Dan and Nettie and Lucy stepped toward the First Class Entrance, the Doorbot had overtaken them and was standing in between them and the doorway.

"I regret, sir, madam, and thing . . ."

"Stop calling me a thing," said Nettie.

"Super Galactic Class Travelers are not allowed beyond this point. Now, if you'd kindly return to your own decks . . ."

"Get out of the way, Jeeves," said Dan and he pushed past the robot.

"Sir will find the door sealed," sniffed the Doorbot, "and

if you do not return to your own quarters I shall be forced to call the ship's security officers. They have vicious rabbits."

Dan and Lucy were by now pushing and pulling on the First Class door, but it was clearly a pointless exercise.

"There must be another way of doing this," said Nettie. Something about her tone of voice made Dan and Lucy calm down and return to rational thinking.

"OK!" said Dan. "Let me handle this. After all, Travel is—or has been—my business. What we have here is the commonest problem known to travelers the world over. How do we get a free upgrade?"

The Doorbot went silent.

"Ha!" Dan recognized the response immediately—corporate dumb insolence. "If you don't tell us how to get a free upgrade immediately I shall report you to the Travel Association." It was a bluff, but it had worked many times before.

"I cannot help you there, *sir*." The contempt in the robot's voice was now so palpable it made your skin feel rough. "You will have to inquire with the Deskbot." And he indicated the desk lamp that Nettie had been talking to earlier.

"Huh!" snorted Nettie. "That machine's about as helpful as a strapless ballgown under g force!"

But Dan had already run over to the Deskbot, and was now preparing to humiliate himself on a heroic scale.

"Look," he began, "we have been misassigned our accommodations. This—as I expect you recognize—is Gloria Stanley, the actress." Dan pointed at Nettie who immediately caught onto his drift and dutifully treated the Deskbot to a sultry look. "I am her manager and this young lady is her lawyer." Lucy really did look the part in her pin-striped power suit. "We should have been given First Class tickets but our travel agent screwed up the booking. Can you reassign us immediately?"

The Deskbot raised its shade or head and stared with its two lamps straight at Dan. He squirmed but held his composure.

"And which travel agency would that be?" asked the Deskbot.

"Top Ten Travel," Dan was well into his role by now.

The Deskbot blinked a few times, as if running through a file somewhere in its database. There was a sort of "bing!" noise and it drummed its fingers on the desk. "I have no record of such an agency in the Galaxy."

"I can assure you it does exist," said Dan, while thinking, "Well, it *did* exist up to this morning."

"Look, we must get an upgrade to First," Lucy had decided to chime in.

"Oh yes, madam," the Deskbot had become insolent-polite. "And to whose account should this 'upgrade' be charged?"

"Mayem, Bader, and Lizt," said Lucy. It was the name of her law firm.

"We have no record of such a company," said the Deskbot.

"You didn't even check your database!" exclaimed Lucy indignantly.

The Deskbot blinked a couple of times and there was another "bing!" noise. The Deskbot leaned forward: "I can only upgrade you if you pay the difference in advance."

"How much is it?" Dan felt they were on a slippery slope here.

"Seventy millon pistres or two pnedes. Currency is not accepted and you may only pay by Galactic Gold Credit Card."

"I don't think you quite appreciate who Gloria Stanley is . . ." Dan decided to change tack.

"I don't give a stuff who 'Gloria Stanley' is," said the Deskbot suddenly and rather surprisingly. "I can only upgrade you if you pay in advance with a Galactic Gold Card."

"Oh, let it go," muttered Nettie, who hated this sort of thing.

"Look," said Lucy in her best lawyer's conciliatory tone, "there must be some way you could organize an upgrade for us. We're valuable customers."

The Deskbot seemed to do a quick check this time on a small screen set in the desk. "Super Galactic Traveler Class— *Complimentary*," it read accusingly. "You're on *free* tickets?!"

"Exactly! We're valued customers! Celebrities!" Dan had thrown caution to the wind. But the Deskbot shook its shade. If it had had a lip, it would have curled.

"I'm sorry, there is absolutely nothing I can do. You

simply cannot upgrade to First Class from Super Galactic Traveler Class—let alone on a *complimentary* ticket. Perhaps if you were Second Class I could do something."

"Look!" said Nettie to the desklight. "We don't care what class we travel . . ."

"I do!" said Dan.

"So do I!" exclaimed Lucy.

"All we want to do," Nettie continued, "is talk to the Captain. Can you put us through to him?"

"It's against company policy," replied the Deskbot, "to allow Super Galactic Class Travelers—especially *complimentary* ones—access to any of the senior officers."

"God!" muttered Nettie to the other two. "I can't stand this. There must be some way of getting through to the Captain."

"How can we get reassigned to Second Class?" Lucy knew now that Dan was well and truly in the grip of that most powerful force known to man: the desire for a free upgrade. Nothing could stop him.

"That, surely, can't be too much to ask?" Dan was halfway between whining and cajoling.

The Deskbot started to look earnestly at the ceiling.

"That's a pretty shade you're wearing." Lucy had decided to try another approach.

"It's just the company colors," said the Deskbot.

"But it suits you," said Lucy.

Dan rolled his eyes.

"Look!" he tried to reassert control on the discussion, but the Deskbot interrupted.

"You have free upgrade vouchers in your rooms. Now *please,* I have better things to do."

10

"Vouchers?" Dan was grunting this as they raced back through the loggia at the top of the Central Well. "Isn't that the Travel Industry all over? Why do they never tell you these things in the first place?"

The Liftbot was in a cheerier mood—but only just. "Down?" it said. "That's what Chalky White yelled at me outside that foxhole at Ypres. It was the last thing he ever did say. Buzz-bomb took him out—same bomb as took out my arm and leg. 'Down!' I can hear his voice to this day . . ."

By the time the elevator had reached the Super Galactic Traveler Class deck, the three had heard a full account of the rudimentary medical facilities available at the Caen dressing station, the technical details of cleaning out gangrene from a deep wound, and a near-complete itemization of the Allied Forces requisitioning techniques in Cyprus. For a robot from a civilization which knew nothing of Earth, it was a very impressive performance.

"God, I just hope we don't have to use that elevator many more times," groaned Dan, as the three raced off down the Super Galactic Traveler Class corridor.

"Primula . . . Dahlia . . . Chrysanthemum . . ." Nettie was reading the names with her translatorspecs.

"We don't even know what ours were called," moaned Lucy.

"Ah! 'Cabbage,'" exclaimed Nettie. "This is mine!"

She gained entry with her PET (Personal Electric Thingie) and found her upgrade voucher on the last page of her copy of the *Super Galactic Traveler Magazine*–just after the Duty-Free Shopping article.

"Look!" she said to the other two. "While you're trying to find your rooms, I'll go and get my upgrade. I've had an idea." She hurried back to the Embarkation Lobby, trying to ignore the Liftbot's account of life on an army pension and no disablement grant, and while the Deskbot reluctantly stamped her ticket with her upgrade to Second Class, she inquired:

"I suppose the Engine Room is aft, is it?"

"At the end of the Grand Axial Canal Second Class, through which you are now entitled to pass. Here is another voucher entitling you to a free glass of Moonswill at the Bar." The Deskbot handed Nettie another ticket and switched itself off.

Nettie went as fast as she could—her high heels echoing round the loggia—toward the entrance to the Second Class Area.

Meanwhile, Lucy and Dan were trailing miserably round the Super Galactic Traveler Class corridors pointing their personal electronic thingies at each door in turn, but to no effect.

"What was Nettie's plan?" Dan decided to take their minds off the present hopeless task.

"She said something about the Engine Room," grunted Lucy.

"Maybe she knows about engines?" said Dan.

"Nettie?! Oh, sure! Hey! There was a click! I swear!" Lucy tried one of the doors, but it was resolutely shut against them.

"Well, you know, for one of Nigel's bimbos that Nettie's pretty bright." Dan nodded to himself.

"Oh, I didn't realize you were interested in her mind," replied Lucy.

"What's that supposed to mean?" Dan was taken by surprise.

"It's opening!" exclaimed Lucy as one door seemed to give for a moment. "Oh! No, it isn't . . ."

"She's a nice girl," said Dan.

"You ought to know. You've been ogling her ever since dinner . . . God! When *was* that? It seems like a lifetime ago!"

"I wasn't ogling her," Dan's "injured innocence" count was incredibly high some days.

"Anyway," Lucy was now working off her frustration, "if Nettie's so bright, how come she allows Nigel to treat her like a Barbie Doll?"

"Does she?"

"That sort of woman makes me sick! Why doesn't she stand up for herself?"

"She still might be quite bright," Dan ventured without much hope. Lucy's powers of certitude always had a crushing effect on him.

"There is no correlation between size of brain and size of breasts," returned Lucy, acidly.

"Got it!" Dan had just pointed his PET at a door and it had, wonderfully and graciously, swung open for them.

"Translatorspecs!" Lucy rapped out her order to the lamp stand, found the *Super Galactic Traveler Magazine* stuck in a rack alongside: a leaflet about aerobics classes, a list of self-operated washing-machine facilities available to Super Galactic Traveler Class passengers, a 132-page form in which to record your personal passenger-satisfaction rating, and a small leaflet entitled "What to Do in the Event of Fire." Evidently the recommended action was to stay extremely calm and remain cool at all times. You were advised to stay in your cabins and not to try and contact any of the staff. And, once again, you were admonished to remain relaxed and enjoy the remainder of the flight.

"Do you think it's getting colder?" asked Lucy as she tore out the voucher from the magazine

"Anyway," said Dan, "I was *not* ogling Nettie."

Nettie shivered as she waited for the door to the Second Class Area to open. For a brief moment she wished her Gap T-Shirt covered her midriff. But then, the door opened and her mind was swamped by the sight before her. She found herself standing on the main jetty of the Grand Axial Canal Second Class. It stretched out in front of her under a simulated sky. Wide columns marked out the elegantly curved walls, and burning braziers dotted the canal embankments. All over the canal, automated gondolas plied lazily back and forth, their robot gondoliers singing pleasantly–a song that brought harmony and peace to the main thoroughfare of the *Starship Titanic*:

"She gave him love!
She swung above!
She kissed him on his smiling, handsome lip.
The gondolier

Sang in her ear:
She gave him six pnedes as a tip!"

Nettie climbed into the nearest gondola and the singing stopped. "Take me to the Engine Room," she said.

"*Si!* Workplace Chum of Victorious Athletics Coach!" said the gondolier and off they drifted down the Grand Axial Canal.

"Tell me," said Nettie. "Shouldn't you be singing when you've got a passenger rather than the other way round?"

"*Si!* Perspicacious Lady Orthodontist!" replied the robot, breathing evenly with the exertion of propelling the craft. "There must be something wrong with the ship's central intelligence system."

Nettie nodded and made a mental note of this.

The gondola took her straight down the very middle of the Grand Axial Canal. The pace was relaxed, and the whole ambience so far away from what she ever imagined being on a spaceship to be like—let alone an *alien* spaceship—that Nettie found herself leaning back against the cushions and letting her mind drift.

She wondered why she didn't feel more distressed by her situation. It was almost as if she felt there was some benign presence in the Starship—something or someone that she knew would take care of them. Nettie shook her head—the thoughts were all a little too shapeless to make sense.

And then what about Nigel? Why didn't she miss him

more? For three months now her whole life had revolved around him. She had made sure his diary was up-to-date and that he looked at it. She'd made him change his socks every day and had washed his underpants by hand. She must love him a lot! And yet she knew he'd just gone out of her life. Not just because they'd been kidnapped by an alien starship full of robots . . . Heavens above! She knew they'd return to Earth. She knew they wouldn't be harmed. But Nigel would not be there for her. Something was broken and yet she didn't seem to regret it.

The gondola bumped. They had reached the jetty.

"The gondolier was on his knees
She blew a kiss from her trapeze . . ."

. . . sang the robot gondolier, as soon as Nettie was out of the gondola.

"Thanks!" said Nettie.

"And that was when the lady lost her grip . . ." sang the robot.

Nettie adjusted her translatorspecs and immediately saw a notice which read: CREW AND PERSONNEL ONLY. She followed the sign down a stainless-steel corridor toward a set of glowing blue doors.

As she approached there was no perceptible engine noise, unless that distant rustling of leaves was it—or was it the beating of a sea upon a distant shore? Nettie felt a thrill pulse through her, and then realized it was just a chill. It really was getting very cold in the ship. And was it her imagination or was her breathing getting more difficult?

At the luminous blue doors, Nettie waved her John Lewis Credit Card and said in a commanding voice that she had never ever used before: "Special Customs and Excise Search Warrant. Open up!"

There was a slight hesitation. The glowing blue doors opened a crack and then shut again, hesitated, and then obediently opened up.

The Engine Room was so similar to the sort of thing you'd see in a science fiction film that Nettie felt she knew exactly where she was. Except what was that black, black darkness behind the thick window? There didn't seem to be anything there and yet all the wiring and so forth seemed to be connected to it.

Nettie looked around for the intercom. Her idea had been quite a simple one: if they couldn't get up to the Bridge to speak to the Captain personally, then she'd telephone him from the Engine Room. There had to be some sort of communication between the Bridge and the Engineers.

In the corner there was a small cabinet. Nettie opened the doors to reveal two buttons. One read: BOMB MONITOR and the other: PRESS TO ARM. A sudden wave of cold, even colder than the current temperature of the ship, swept through Nettie's body. "Bomb!?" Was there a bomb on board?

Nettie pressed the button that read BOMB MONITOR.

A polite voice said: "Thank you for inquiring about the status of the Mega-Scuttler Company's 8D-96 Full Force Mega-Scuttler–'A Bomb to Be Proud Of'–which has been installed, for your convenience, upon this starship. It is my pleasure to inform you that the Mega-Scuttler is currently not activated. Thank you for showing an interest in bombs."

"Bit of a relief," muttered Nettie. "Now where's the intercom?"

What happened next is totally unclear. Certainly Nettie herself had no recollection. She remembered climbing up the ladder next to the armor-plated window. She could recall feeling colder than ever and finding it harder to breathe and then feeling a force gripping her . . . a force pulling her sideways off the ladder . . . a force so vast that she thought she was being sucked into a Black Hole or something . . . as she felt herself falling horizontally off the ladder toward whatever it was behind the perspex window. . . . The next thing she knew she was whirling around in blackness–fighting for her life.

II

Dan and Lucy were having trouble.

They had both procured their vouchers and had successfully wheedled an upgrade to Second Class out of the Deskbot, but the trickier negotiation for an upgrade to First Class was proving to be a remarkably harrowing experience.

"You have no Credit Card. You are not members of the Sixty Million Miles Club. You are not even registered Frequent Travelers! This whole discussion is pointless. You will find the Second Class facilities on board this starship more than adequate for *your* requirements."

How could even a robot be so unbelievably, unremittingly snotty? wondered Dan.

"Dan!" said Lucy. "We're wasting our breath–in fact, is it my imagination or is it getting harder to breathe?"

Dan sniffed the air. Lucy was right. It was also getting colder. "Jesus!" he muttered.

"The air and heating are at normal levels," announced a Doorbot.

"That's bullshit!" snapped Lucy. "It's getting colder and it's getting more difficult to breathe!"

"I can assure you that the air supply and the temperature are set to maximum for Super Galactic Traveler Class comfort," said the Doorbot.

"Are you trying to tell us there are different levels of air supply for the different classes of traveler!" exclaimed Dan.

"Not normally, sir, no," replied the Doorbot. "However, should the ship be traveling without First or Second Class passengers, the oxygen and heating will, naturally, be lowered to the comfort requirements of Super Galactic Traveler Class passengers."

"Jesus!" exclaimed Lucy. "You guys are the most cynical bunch I have ever come across!"

"I'm going straight to the Travel Association when I get home!" Dan was not messing about any longer! He was now beginning to sweat with panic–despite the cold. "There isn't enough air to breathe!"

"There is ample air and heat for the Super Galactic

Traveler decks, sir, but unfortunately it is getting dispersed over the whole ship."

Lucy, meanwhile, was back at the Deskbot, hammering on the desk.

"I'm sorry, madam," the Deskbot was saying, "but it is company policy to supply First and Second Class air and heat only if there are First and Second Class passengers on board."

"But *we're* Second Class passengers!"

"I have no record of any Second Class passengers on board."

"But you just gave us an upgrade! We had vouchers!"

"I'm afraid Second Class vouchers are not processed until the end of the month. Thank you for your inquiry." The Deskbot suddenly turned itself off.

"All right . . . All right . . ." Dan was trying to work himself round to Decisive Mode. "It's vital we all stick together. Go and get Nettie, while I try and sort this mess out."

"But if I go and get Nettie, we won't be all sticking together." Lucy's rational streak tended to obtrude whenever Dan was in Decisive Mode.

"All right! I'll go and get her."

"That's the same thing! Anyway, why are you so worried about Nettie?"

"I'm not! I just think we all ought to keep together in case one of us needs help."

"Like what sort of help do we give if we're all running

out of air and freezing to death?" Lucy was getting quite steamed up considering the cold.

"All right! Don't go and look for Nettie! But what *are* we going to do?"

Dan sounded so desperate, so forlorn . . . and yet, oddly, Lucy preferred it to Decisive Mode.

"I'll see if I can find a supply of oxygen. You get us up to First Class!"

"But that's still not 'sticking together'!" moaned Dan.

"I never said we *should* stick together. That was your idea," said Lucy. Then she put her arms round Dan and gave him a big kiss on the cheek. She couldn't resist Dan when he seemed vulnerable. "Cheer up, Second Class Traveler! I'm sure we're going to be all right!" And with that she had gone, and Dan suddenly felt terribly alone.

So alone . . . he felt he could pick his loneliness up in his hands and hug it . . . but even as he felt this, he realized it wasn't the absence of Lucy that made him feel empty inside. It was something else.

12

Lucy had a good brain even though she had lived all her life in L.A. Despite the continual exposure to carbon monoxide and people from the film industry, she had remained smart. She had trained as a lawyer and was well-regarded in the firm where she practiced. Her speciality was entertainment law, but she still liked to use that brain of hers, and here was a good opportunity.

"Where would they keep the oxygen equipment?" She actually said it aloud as she paced across the loggia at the top of the Central Well. "Got it!" Suddenly she knew exactly where to look. God! It was so great to be bright! She'd always thanked her stars that she hadn't been born a busty bimbo like some people she could think of.

"A department store," she told herself, "would have a plan of the store by the elevators . . . So . . ." And sure enough—there it was! By the elevators—even though this wasn't a department store. She pressed a small button, and a large area of the floor lit up displaying the plan of the *Starship Titanic*. What's more, she could zoom in and out with a second control. This was better than anything they had at Macy's!

Lucy slipped on her translatorspecs and read: MEDICAL CENTER. That was where she'd find oxygen. And without waiting to take advantage of any of the special offers the plan of the ship assured Second Class Passengers they would be delighted with, she hurried toward the Starship's Medical Center.

The Medical Center of the *Starship Titanic* took up a whole four-hundred-yard section of the main hull—under the Embarkation Level. It was dazzlingly new and clean and it said: "Hello, and welcome to the Medical Center of the *Starship Titanic*. A place to enjoy and savor the Good Things of Life while you still have it—not just somewhere to be sick! We guarantee you will feel no pain once you have placed your credit card in our Card Care Machine!"

"Jesus!" thought Lucy. "Could they do with a new copywriter!" Her breathing was all the time becoming a little more difficult, and it was noticeably colder. She looked around for anything that might resemble an oxygen cylinder and suddenly froze in a way that had nothing to do with the temperature.

Unlike the rest of the ship, the Medical Center was not unpopulated. There were two people—or *were* they people? There were two *figures* on the floor, and one of them was looking straight at her. Lucy stared back. Somehow she knew, without a shadow of a doubt, that he was not human. He *looked* human enough, but there was a curious "otherness" about him. It was intangible . . . subtle . . . intriguing . . . Then she noticed he had the most beautiful orange eyes. . . .

Lucy screamed and turned to escape, but the alien had already leapt to its feet, and the door of the Medical Center had closed behind her. In her panic, she couldn't figure out how to open it again.

A powerful arm gripped her around the neck, and a voice that sent a shiver right through her said: "Don't struggle. I can break your neck."

Lucy went kind of limp. She always claimed she didn't actually faint, but The Journalist, for this is who had his arm around her neck, later said he dragged her over to the nearest bed and láid her out unconscious for several minutes.

When Lucy came round, she saw her bloodstained assailant bent over a dead body. She realized immediately he was a crazed killer searching through his victim's clothes—

such odd clothes, Lucy noticed: strange colors, strange cut, strange materials . . . It was at this point that she also realized she was tied down to the bed.

The full horror of her situation suddenly hit her like a forty-ton truck hitting a shop window: she was shattered and her alarm went off. "Aaaaaarggh! Aarrrrrgrh! Arggggggggh!" screamed Lucy.

The Journalist looked across at her and clicked his teeth in annoyance.

"Shut up!" he snarled.

Oh my God! The Murderer had spoken to her! Here she was, a defenseless woman, tied to a bed, waiting for this violent sadist to finish rifling the pockets of his last victim and then come across to her and do . . . do what . . . do whatever he likes! That's what! To *her*! To Lucy Webber—a graduate of UCLA law school!

"Aaaaaaaaaargh! Arrrrrrrgh! Aaaaarggggghhh!" Lucy had never screamed so well or so effectively in her life. Unfortunately, the effect was not to bring Dan running to her rescue but to attract the unwanted attentions of her murderous assailant.

He came across and stared into her eyes. The screams died on Lucy's lips as she registered the cruel twist of his mouth and the sadistic glint in those beautiful orange-colored eyes. The next moment she saw his bloodstained hand move to cover her mouth.

"Listen!" said the Psychopath. "There's a bomb on board

this ship! It's going to explode and take us with it unless I can find it quick! So just SHUT UP with the screaming—I can't think and it makes me crazy!"

God! thought Lucy, it was just like one of those films, where the heroine is captured by the serial killer–rapist and yet finds herself strangely drawn to him. "What am I thinking about?!" Lucy suddenly brought herself up short. "Aaaaaah! Aaargh!" Screaming really seemed the only sensible alternative.

"Didn't you hear what I said?" The Killer-Rapist was now glaring into her eyes once again. Lucy felt her bowels go soft with fear, and her breath grew even scarcer than it was. "There is a bomb. I have to find the bomb."

Lucy went quiet, and thought about this. A bomb was clearly not good news.

The murderer returned to his victim and continued examining his pockets—of which there were rather a lot. Scraliontis had always been an expensive dresser, and you could always reckon on his suits having more pockets than anyone else's—that being the fashion of the day.

"Suffering Supernovae!" thought The Journalist. "I've never seen so many pockets!"

"Why are you doing that?" Lucy surprised herself with the steadiness of her voice.

"I'm looking to see if he's got anything to show where the bomb is," said The Journalist.

"Why should he have?" asked Lucy.

"Stop asking questions," snapped The Journalist.

"I just asked why?"

"Because he planted the bomb."

"Oh," said Lucy. "Thank you." And then thought: "Why on Earth am I being polite to someone who's just about to kill me? Maybe even rape me first! Or maybe he isn't." Maybe there were mitigating circumstances. Maybe the Psychopath wasn't a psychopath? Maybe he was a caring family man with a flair for initiating excitement, who was resourceful in danger and yet prepared to submit to the will of a strong and loving woman . . .

"Is that why you killed him?" Lucy felt surprisingly childish asking the question. "Because he planted the bomb?"

"I didn't kill him!"

Suddenly Lucy saw her murderer-to-be in a new light. For a start, maybe he wasn't a murderer. In the second place, she noticed he was hurt himself; he seemed to be in some pain as he bent over the body. Perhaps he wasn't going to rape or kill her either.

"Haaaa!" The Journalist gave a yell that made Lucy jump.

"Have you got it?" Lucy asked nervously.

"Shut up!" said The Journalist. He had a small piece of paper which he was now stuffing into one of his many pockets (although he didn't have nearly as many as Scraliontis).

"Hey! Hey! You can't leave me here!" Lucy had gone from abject terror to incensed indignation in less time than most people could go from feeling OK to still feeling OK.

"I can't waste time!" snapped The Journalist. "It may go off any second!" And he made for the door.

"DON'T LEAVE ME TIED UP IN HERE WITH A DEAD BODY!" screamed Lucy. Something in her tone of voice—maybe the sheer volume of it—made The Journalist stop. He turned and looked at Lucy, in her power pinstripe, tied to the bed, her black hair falling across her face.

"Shit!" he said. The actual Blerontin phrase was: "North of Pangalin," which was a particularly unpleasant suburb of Blerontis, the capital of Blerontin, but the meaning was: "Shit!"

He limped over to the bed and untied Lucy.

"Just don't get in the way," he said.

"Don't talk to me like that!" fired Lucy.

"Oh! You're going to be a great help! I can see that!" replied The Journalist as he set off down the corridor toward the stairs up to the Embarkation Level.

"Wait!" Lucy shouted after him. "I've got to find a supply of oxygen!"

"Forget it!"

"But it's getting hard to breathe!"

"Not as hard as it will be once we're tiny fragments floating in space!" retorted The Journalist.

Lucy was by now running alongside him. "You're an alien, aren't you?" she suggested, as they waited for the Doorbot to open the door to the Second Class Area.

"No," replied The Journalist. "You're the alien. This is a Blerontinian starship in case you hadn't noticed."

"Point taken," said Lucy. Dan would never have talked to her like this. "Oh my God!" she exclaimed as the doors opened and she took in for the first time the majestic sweep of the Grand Axial Canal Second Class.

"She plumett-ed
And hit his head
And gave him six pnedes as a tip!"

. . . sang the gondoliers.

"Ohh!" The Journalist gasped as he stepped down into the nearest gondola, and missed his footing. Lucy caught him and held him for a moment.

"You're hurt," she said.

"Let's get on!" he returned. "We have no idea when the bomb is timed to go off."

Lucy helped him down into the gondola, and the singing stopped.

"Take us to the Engine Room," gasped The Journalist, holding his stomach.

"Si! Si! Nitrogen-Loathing Respecters of Pressed Veal!"

"And make it fast."

"Si! Si!"

The gondola set off down the Great Canal at no greater speed than any other. Lucy looked across at her former assailant: he was rocking backwards and forwards, hugging himself.

"Are you cold?" asked Lucy. She certainly was. But The Journalist didn't reply; he just gritted his teeth and Lucy suddenly realized he was in real pain.

"What happened?" she asked, and touched his arm.

"That bastard—Scraliontis—stabbed me with a table lamp," growled the ex-murderer.

Lucy stifled a laugh. "How can you stab someone with a . . ."

"It had a sharp end," interrupted The Journalist.

"Are you in pain?" asked Lucy. The Journalist grunted. Lucy leaned toward him and moved his hands away from his stomach. The unfamiliar smell of a being from another world caught her unawares—it was not unpleasant, quite the contrary, but it made her head spin.

"Leave me alone!" he growled.

"Let me look at it." Lucy pushed him back onto the pillow and tried to open his clothes where the congealed blood was thickest. "I have no idea how to undo this," she said.

"Thought-seal," he said, and suddenly the garment opened so that Lucy was able to pull it back and reveal The Journalist's gouged flesh.

"Oh! It's nasty!" she said. "Look!" Suddenly she made a quick movement. The Journalist yelled, and she pulled a large shard of glass from his abdomen. The blood welled up again from the wound.

"I couldn't see it!" he gasped. "Thanks!" And he held up a small packet. "Here!" he said.

"Oh! Thank you!" said Lucy, accepting the gift in what she felt was an appropriately gracious way. "What is it?"

"A plaster," said The Journalist. "Stick it on before I bleed to death."

"A lady, she say we ought to sing while passengers are in the gondola and not other way round," confided the gondolabot, clearly feeling the need for a bit of small-talk. "We think something maybe seriously wrong."

"Just get us to the Engine Room!"

13

By the time they had reached the Engine Room, Lucy had managed to convince The Journalist that her name really was Lucy.

"But you know what that means in Blerontin?" The Journalist was in some pain from the laughter. He'd managed to stop at last, and Lucy was feeling a bit piqued.

"No," she said coldly. "What does it mean?"

"I can't tell you," he replied.

"I'd like to know."

"No no no no no—I just couldn't!"

"What's so funny? Go on, you've got to tell me!"

"Maybe when I know you better—oh! argh! ha ha ha! It hurts!"

"Well, what's your name?" she asked.

"The Journalist," replied The Journalist.

"That's not a name, that's a job description," objected Lucy.

The Journalist shrugged. "On Blerontin newshacks aren't allowed individual names—it's an ancient law—something to do with avoiding the cult of the personality or something."

"I can't call you The Journalist!"

"Just call me 'The,'" he said, and opened the luminous blue doors of the Engine Room.

A quick look inside drew his attention immediately to the small cabinet in the corner. The Journalist strode straight across to it, opened the doors, glanced at the two buttons, and without hesitation pressed the one marked: PRESS TO ARM.

Immediately a flap opened and a large black steel egg with fins rose up out of the top of the cabinet. At the same time a voice boomed out: "You have just activated the 8D-96 Full Force Mega-Scuttler—'A Bomb to Be Proud Of'—created especially for you by the Mega-Scuttler Corporation of Dormillion. This will be a fairly big explosion so please stand well back—about twenty-two thousand miles. Countdown to detonation commencing at once. One thousand . . . nine hundred ninety-nine . . . nine hundred ninety-eight . . . nine hundred ninety-seven."

Lucy couldn't believe what she'd just witnessed. She looked at the two buttons again through her translatorspecs. "Why, for crying out loud, did you press the button that says: 'Press to Arm'?" she exclaimed.

The Journalist was hopping round the Engine Room kicking himself.

"I didn't know it was a Dormillion bomb!"

"What difference does it make? A bomb's a bomb!"

"I can't explain!"

"I need to know!" insisted Lucy.

"No you don't!"

He was perfectly right. Lucy, herself, wondered why she was pressing this point. She grabbed hold of The Journalist's shoulders and shook him.

"Look, you stupid jerk! You've just done something really idiotic and I have a right to know why!"

"All right!" The Journalist seemed to calm down. "It's just that the Dormillion for 'Press to Arm' is very similar to the Blerontin for 'Please Press Dog.' It was just a simple mistranslation!" he groaned. "I was wondering what the dog had to do with it!"

"Great!" said Lucy. "So now we really are up shit's creek without a bucket!"

"Nine hundred ninety-three . . . nine hundred ninety-two . . . nine hundred ninety-one," continued the bomb.

"WHAT ARE WE GOING TO DO?!" she yelled.

"We're going to keep calm," said The Journalist.

"Good thinking, 'The'!" snorted Lucy summing up her not inconsiderable reserves of sarcasm. "You clearly have a mind the size of Arnold Schwarzenegger's humeral ligament! We're running out of oxygen. The temperature's rapidly becoming suitable for an arctic winter on Pluto! You've just activated what was otherwise a harmless bomb and *now* you have the nerve to tell *me* to stay calm!"

"Who's Arnold Schwarzenegger?" asked The Journalist.

"Arrrrghhhhhhh!" Lucy decided that a good scream was probably the wisest course of action under the circumstances.

The Journalist suddenly screamed as well. Lucy looked at him. "I'm sorry," he said. "It's just I can't think when you do that."

"I'm sorry, too." Lucy felt stupid. The Journalist smiled, and then, for no apparent reason, gave her a kiss on the cheek. Lucy was so surprised to be kissed by an alien with beautiful orange eyes, she simply stood there, and heard him say:

"The clock is counting once every innim! That gives us about sixteen edoes before it gets to zero!"

"How long's an innim?" Lucy wanted to say but her mouth wasn't working. All she could do was stare into those strange and beautiful eyes as she heard him say:

"What we must do is find the lifeboats!"

Dan was still deep in argument with the desk lamp in the Embarkation Lobby. It was an argument he had become familiar with over the years of Top Ten Travel. But there was something wrong. Somehow he just wasn't getting his points across. This damned desk lamp seemed to be coming out on top every time. Then Dan realized his problem was air—or rather the lack of air—he just wasn't getting the amount of oxygen into his brain that a travel agent needs to argue for a free upgrade.

He was panting and gasping. He was also on his knees and his head was beginning to spin.

"If you want me to go to the Press and blow this story up, I'm quite happy to do so . . ." He knew once you were reduced to this line of attack the cause was probably lost. They'd never get into First Class, they'd never get to the Captain, and they'd all die of asphyxiation and cold. Great.

At that moment, he heard footsteps running across the loggia of the Central Well and an exhausted Lucy, accompanied by a strange man with bright orange eyes, staggered into the Embarkation Lobby. The two of them collapsed next to Dan and lay there trying to get their breath.

"Who's this?" Dan was surprisingly indignant for someone who was in the process of dying of asphyxiation.

"Bomb!" gasped The Journalist.

"You're a bomb?" said Dan.

"No!" Lucy felt she had to explain. "The, this is Dan. Dan, this is The."

Dan blinked a few times.

"There's a bomb on board! It's about to go off!" The

Journalist managed to get out. "We've got to get to the lifeboats!"

"They're in First Class!" explained Lucy. "Naturally."

"Now *that* is outrageous!" Dan received this new ammunition gratefully and turned on the Deskbot. "If I tell the Travel Association *that*, they'll blacklist your whole fleet forever!" Wow! That was some threat! Dan knew; they'd had it leveled against the Top Ten Travel Co., Inc., countless times.

The Deskbot tapped its fingers on the desk and gazed up at the ceiling.

"D'you hear?" exclaimed Dan. "I'll close this whole god-damned company down!"

"Listen, you Dumbbot!" The Journalist had grabbed the Deskbot by its scrawny stand. "This is a matter of life and death! There's a bomb about to go off in . . ." He checked his watch. "In ten edoes! Pangalin!"

"How long's that?" asked Dan, but The Journalist wasn't listening. He was too busy shaking the robot. Suddenly there was a crack and a flash and all the lights went off for an instant.

"Hey!" cried everyone, and the lights came on again—although there was no cause and effect between the shout of "Hey!" and the recommencement of illumination.

"I'm sorry. There is nothing I can do unless you have a Galactic Gold Credit Card," replied the robot in a simulated strangled voice.

"Pangalin!" repeated The Journalist.

"Please mind your language," croaked the Deskbot.

"Don't you have a credit card, The?" asked Lucy, appalled to think her new friend might not be the most solvent character on Blerontin.

"Not a Galactic Gold!" he said.

"Who *is* this?" Dan had switched back to Indignation Mode.

"You've got to earn over seven pnedes a week to get one of those beauties!" The Journalist was still trying to strangle the Deskbot.

"It's getting really hard to breathe!" choked Lucy.

Ice was now forming on the edge of the desk. Dan pointed at it: "You call that Super Galactic Class comfort?!" He choked.

"Take your hands off my flex!" choked the Deskbot. "You'll short me again!"

"Get us into First Class NOW!" choked The Journalist. "Or I'll smash your lampshade!"

Lucy had collapsed on the floor, and Dan rushed to her. "Where did you find that guy?" he whispered into her ear.

"Save . . . your . . . breath . . ." panted Lucy.

"Help!" screamed the Deskbot. "Security!"

"May you rot in Pangalin!" yelled The Journalist.

It was at that moment that an extraordinary thing happened. Or, rather, it was at that moment that an extraordinary thing crawled into the Embarkation Lobby, across the highly polished floor, and up to the Deskbot.

It was clearly alive—although only just—and it was very old, very very very old. It was wizened and blackened. In its twiglike fingers the creature held a Personal Electronic Thingie. It waved this under the Deskbot's nose and croaked in an ancient voice: "Upgrade . . . all of us!"

The Deskbot immediately sprang to attention and became perceptibly brighter.

"Of course, madam! What a pleasure to welcome you to the First Class facilities of the *Starship Titanic*. You will find them without equal anywhere in the Galaxy! Please go through and have a pleasant trip!"

There was a hiss of air returning to the cabins and an instant rise in temperature, as the ship registered the arrival of four First Class passengers. The door to the First Class Area swung open and Dan and Lucy, The Journalist and the Ancient Creature, stepped through into another, and even more amazing, world.

14

"Nettie!" exclaimed Dan. "My God! You're Nettie! What's happened to you?" But the Ancient Creature, who Dan had rightly diagnosed as Nettie, couldn't reply. The moment they passed into the First Class Section, she collapsed and lay as if dead. The Gap T-shirt hung around her shrunken frame like an overlarge pullover. Her jewelry looked foolish and ill-advised on her scrawny wrists and neck. What on Earth—or off the Earth—had happened to her?

What had, in fact, happened, was this.

The *Starship Titanic* was powered by the

latest and most incredible invention of the great Leovinus's genius. No one knew how he had done it, and he had kept it an absolute secret, but somehow he had harnessed for the Starship—his beloved masterpiece—the vastest source of power in the probable Universe: a captive Black Hole.

Naturally, something as powerful as a Black Hole needed very careful handling and had to be surrounded by incredible safety precautions. Unfortunately, safety was one thing that neither Scraliontis nor Brobostigon had had first in their minds when they began to reduce the specifications for the construction of the ship.

"There won't *be* anybody in the Engine Room," explained Scraliontis, when even Brobostigon had queried the wisdom of reducing the Incredibly Strong Glass Company's spec. for the observation window onto the Black Hole.

"But you know what Black Holes are like . . ."

Actually, Scraliontis didn't; he was an accountant and not an engineer. In any case, Black Hole Technology was a brand-new concept straight out of Leovinus's brain. "Just take Leovinus's lowest parameter for the glass shield!" he snapped. "We can't afford any more."

It was Nettie who discovered the problem thus caused by Scraliontis's cost-cutting, as she climbed the ladder, looking for the phone to the Captain's Bridge. The force of the Black Hole had simply plucked her off the ladder and absorbed her through the Incredibly Strong Glass Company's below-spec. window.

Once in the Black Hole, she had begun to spin around for—as far as her body was concerned—hundreds of years, traveling millions of light-years round in tiny circles. Fortunately, she still had her Personal Electronic Thingie on her, and this had dutifully clocked up all the miles she traveled.

Nettie herself didn't know how she had escaped. In fact, she had been thrown clear of the Black Hole when The Journalist had short-circuited the Deskbot. Nettie was, miraculously, still alive, and, even more miraculously, still had the presence of mind to realize that she had accumulated millions of light-years of SpaceMiles—enough to get them all free upgrades to First Class.

"Less than eight edoes to go!" exclaimed The Journalist. "And that's assuming the bomb doesn't speed up its counting!"

"What can I do about Nettie?" cried Dan, holding the Ancient Creature pathetically in his arms.

"Leave her! We've got to find the lifeboats!" And The Journalist was off, running along the embankment of the Grand Axial Canal First Class, with Lucy in close pursuit.

"Come on, Dan!" she called.

"I can't just leave her!" Dan yelled back. But they'd turned a corner and were gone. Dan tried to lift the ancient Nettie up, but even though she was emaciated and shriveled, he was too exhausted to carry her anywhere.

He looked around and, for the first time, took in the extraordinary vista presented by the Grand Axial Canal First

Class. If the word "posh" ever had any meaning, this was it. It was luxury. It was Deluxe. It was Expensive. It was also redolent with the operatic singing of the gondolabots:

"He helped to chalk
Her tightrope walk
So that the lovely lady wouldn't slip . . ."

Dan had always hated opera. "Let's go somewhere quiet," he whispered to Nettie, and finally lifted her up and staggered into the nearest doorway.

Lucy and The Journalist had, meanwhile, discovered that the Star-Struct Construction Co., Inc., had not skimped on the signs to the lifeboats (First Class). There were big reassuring signs almost everywhere you looked. They were illuminated and some of them incorporated flashing arrows. Consequently, the two arrived at the Lifeboat Assembly Station in less than a minute.

"Seven innims to go!" gasped The Journalist.

As he said this, both he and Lucy discovered that while the Star-Struct Construction Co., Inc., hadn't skimped on the signs to the lifeboats, they *had* economized on the lifeboats themselves. In fact, they had economized completely and utterly on them.

"Well, what's the point of providing lifeboats," Scraliontis had reasoned to an increasingly nervous Brobostigon, "if there aren't going to be any passengers?"

"The bastards!" groaned The Journalist.

"That's it!" said Lucy.

"We're done for! We'll be blown to little bits of drifting cosmos in exactly six edoes forty-five innims!" The Journalist sank to his knees. The fight had gone out of him. He looked so helpless, so forlorn. Lucy couldn't help it. The thought of imminent destruction threw all the usual caution out of her mind. She leapt to a conclusion that she would probably not even have begun to recognize under normal conditions.

"Oh, God!" she cried. "I love you!"

And before The Journalist realized what was happening, Lucy was all over him, kissing his mouth and running her fingers through his hair.

"Ow! Ouch!" The Journalist yelled. "Mind my wound!"

"I'm sorry! I'm sorry!" yelled Lucy. "But we've only got six edoes left! Whatever they are! I've never felt like this for *anyone*. . . . The moment I set eyes on you . . . Oh, God! No one's ever going to know! Nothing matters anymore! But hurry! Do something!" And she was wrestling with his clothing. "I can't get it off!"

"I told you! It's thought-sealed!" His clothes suddenly pinged open and the next minute Lucy had flung her pinstriped power suit onto the empty lifeboat ramp. Her fingers ran over the alien's body, as she got on top of him.

"Oh, God!" she cried, feeling the blood draining down into her lower abdomen like a rush of seagulls onto the last herring. "We've probably only got five of whatever those things are left!"

"Edoes!" The Journalist tried not to yell out with the pain of his wound. "We've got five edoes left! This is incredible!" he cried. "We don't do it like this on Blerontin!"

"Why not?" Lucy didn't care.

"It's illegal!" The Journalist was grinning from ear to ear. "We're only allowed 'snork-style'! You know—upside down, from above!"

"Oh shut up!" Lucy was kissing him. "I had to tell you! I had to! I love you! I've always loved you! That's what's been missing! Ah! Ah!"

"Quick!" cried The Journalist. They had only sixty innims before the bomb exploded.

"Yes! Yes!"

They rolled and kissed each other, oblivious to the cold metal floor of the lifeboat ramp under their naked flesh. "Life is so short!" Lucy suddenly grabbed his hand and looked at his watch. It was totally incomprehensible. "What's it say?" she asked.

"Thirty innims!"

"Is that all?" she yelled.

"Yes!" cried The Journalist. "Yes!"

"I love yooooou!" cried Lucy.

"Ooooooooh!" cried The Journalist and the two of them collapsed together as the clock clicked to zero. . . .

They lay there waiting for the forever-ending explosion that would terminate their brief affair. But, unlike the two lovers, it didn't come.

"What's happened?" Lucy was the first to speak.

"I don't know?" said The Journalist. "I don't know!"

15

•

At this same moment, Nettie suddenly managed to sit up on the couch, on which Dan had placed her, and screamed: "Oh my God! There's only five minutes before the bomb goes off!"

"Five minutes!" thought Dan. "This is where, in a cheap novel, the couple, confronted by imminent oblivion, would suddenly make passionate love." It was a pity Nettie was now as old as she was.

"You've got to go and talk to it!" she pleaded.

"What?" said Dan.

"I can't explain! Just believe me! It's in the Engine Room! Hurry!"

"What?" repeated Dan a bit gormlessly.

"HURRY! THE ENGINE ROOM! SPEAK TO THE BOMB!"

Dan decided that, while gormlessness had its place in the human repertoire of reactions, now was neither the time nor place for it. He sprinted out of the Beauty Salon (which was, apparently, where they were) and ran down the length of the Grand Axial Canal, trying to ignore the inevitable chorus:

"She threw her arms
Around his charms,
And gave him six pnedes as a tip!"

The first thing he saw, when he burst into the Engine Room, was a large bomb sticking up out of a cabinet. A friendly sort of voice was booming out:

"Fifty-eight . . . fifty-seven . . . fifty-six . . . fifty-five . . . fifty-four . . ."

Dan couldn't think what to say. After all, he'd never addressed a bomb before. He didn't have a clue what sort of thing it would be interested in.

"Hello," he said.

"Fifty-three . . . fifty-two . . . hello . . . fifty-one . . . fifty . . ." replied the bomb genially.

"Any chance of you not exploding?" Dan thought he might as well get straight to the point.

"No . . . forty-eight . . . forty-seven . . ."

Dan was not the most imaginative of men. He knew it. Lucy knew it. Nigel had known it. He was dedicated, hard-working, loyal, thorough—all those admirable and desirable things for anybody's partner to be. But leaps of the imagination were not his forte. And yet, he had one now. He suddenly knew the one thing that bombs were bound to be interested in.

"Do you really want to do this?" he asked. "I mean, isn't it a bit self-destructive?"

"Forty-six . . . forty-five . . . forty—Look! I am just a simple counting and exploding device and am not equipped for philosophical discourse," replied the bomb. "Please do not speak to me while I'm counting. Damn! Now you've made me lose my place! You see? Recommencing countdown. One thousand . . . nine hundred ninety-nine . . . nine hundred ninety-eight . . ."

"Got the sucker!" thought Dan. He checked his watch against the bomb's counting. They had about sixteen minutes before they needed to talk to it again. He turned and raced back to Nettie.

As he ran, the thought of Nettie kept riffling his mind like a gambler's hands riffling a deck of cards. God! She was so intelligent! How had she learned the bomb's weakness so quickly? The clarity of her intellect made him feel so ordinary and humble.

But then he suddenly remembered how she seemed

old and shriveled: he must have been seeing things! That couldn't have happened to the beautiful, gorgeous Nettie? And yet, it was then that Dan found himself thinking the most curious thought: of course, it was terrible if something *had* happened to Nettie (and what *had* happened to her?) but at least now, thought Dan, he might stand a chance of winning her!

Lucy was putting her clothes on rather hurriedly. The fact that she and The Journalist had not been blown to cosmic dust had acutely embarrassed her. In fact, she didn't know where to look.

The Journalist was regarding her curiously. "You do things very differently in your world," he said.

"Oh?" Lucy tried to pretend that everything was perfectly normal.

"Yes," he said. "On Blerontin we have all these absurd rituals we have to go through before having sex. There's a thing called dating, when a young couple go out for evenings together without necessarily 'going the whole way,' as we say. Then there's a thing called the engagement, where rings are exchanged. Finally there's an elaborate ceremony called a wedding, with a cake and 'bridesmaids' and the 'best man's speech'—not to mention the 'honeymoon'! You wouldn't believe the rigmarole we have to go through in order to make love to each other. I like your Earth way of doing it much better."

"The bomb still might go off at any second!" Lucy reminded him.

"The bomb? Oh! Pangalin! I'd forgotten!" The Journalist thought-sealed his clothes.

As they raced down the Grand Axial Canal Second Class, they didn't realize that they had missed bumping into Dan on his way back to the Beauty Salon by exactly one eight-hundred-and-sixty-fourth of a second, which, by an incredible coincidence, was exactly where the bomb had got to in its countdown, when Lucy and The Journalist arrived back in the Engine Room.

"Eight hundred sixty-four ... eight hundred sixty-three ..." said the bomb.

"Why's it only got as far as eight hundred sixty-three?" wondered Lucy.

"You're beautiful!" replied The Journalist.

Lucy became aware that he was still looking at her in a rather odd way, and she suddenly wished he'd concentrate on the problem at hand.

"Maybe it doesn't count when we're out of the room?" she suggested. She pulled her companion out of the door, but as she started to listen, Lucy suddenly felt the alien's hands around her breasts.

"Ohh! Lucy! I can't stop thinking about you!" he murmured as he nuzzled her neck.

"Eight hundred sixty-two ... eight hundred sixty-one . . ." continued the bomb even though they were out of the room. That was one theory out of the way, thought Lucy, disentangling herself from The Journalist's embrace.

Back in the room, she stared at the bomb and tried to think, but it was hard with an alien sticking his tongue in her ear and saying he loved her more than anything in his world.

"Please, The!" exclaimed Lucy. "We haven't got time for that now . . ."

"You started it . . ." he reminded her. "Once we're roused, us Blerontinian males tend to be very single-minded."

"I've met your type before," said Lucy, trying to push him away.

"Just put your hands on that bit again!" he was whispering in her ear.

"Stop it!" cried Lucy.

"What?" replied the bomb. "Oh damn! I thought you were talking to me! Now you've made me lose count! Recommencing countdown, One thousand . . . nine hundred ninety-nine . . ."

"I love you!" said The Journalist. "You're all I've ever dreamed about."

"It lost count!" exclaimed Lucy.

"Please put your hand here . . ." said The Journalist.

"Listen!" cried Lucy to the bomb. "Which baseball team won the World Series in 1997?"

"Nine hundred ninety-seven . . . nine hundred ninety— now I've told you before about interrupting me while I'm in the middle of a countdown. If you want a bomb you can have a good natter with you should have got the Mega-Scuttler Pro, which has multitasking, speech recognition, and general chattering software and therefore makes an altogether more expensive bang. As it is, you've got me, and I'm doing my best under increasingly trying circumstances. Recommencing countdown. One thousand ... Nine hundred ninety-nine ..."

"You have the most wonderful skin," moaned The Journalist, biting Lucy quite hard on the earlobe.

"Ouch!" cried Lucy. "Look, The, you've got to stay here and keep talking to the bomb while I go up and find the Captain's Bridge."

"I can't bear to be separated from you!" he clutched at her arm.

"If you don't stay and talk to the bomb we're both going to get blown up!" she replied.

"Just let's do it once more!" pleaded The Journalist. "I'll be able to think properly then. Honestly! Blerontinian males need to have sex at least twice before they can think straight. It's well known!"

Lucy sighed, brushed the alien's hair straight and wondered what on Earth she'd got herself into. . . .

16

While Dan had gone to talk to the bomb, the prematurely aged Nettie had taken the opportunity to look around the room in which she found herself. At first she thought it must be some sort of torture chamber or at least an interrogation room. But once she'd put on her translatorspecs, she realized she was in the ship's Hair Dressing Salon and Beauty Parlor. The thumbscrews were actually elaborate nailclippers, the electric chairs were highly ergonomic sitting structures, and the individual gas chambers were hair dryers. It was obvious once you read the motto over the doorway:

WELCOME TO THE *STARSHIP TITANIC* BEAUTY THERAPY AND HAIR CREATIONRY. YOU WILL LEAVE HERE LOVELIER AND YOUNGER.

Nettie put out a wizened finger and pressed the button on the wall beside the couch marked: PRESS FOR SERVICE. A metal cage on an articulated arm suddenly sprang up over the back of the couch and dangled a few inches in front of her face. At the same time, a large glass case began to descend from the ceiling until both she and the couch were encompassed by it. A reassuring voice then said:

"We have assessed your beauty requirements and, while recognizing you have a severe problem, we would like to reassure you that there is nothing you can wish to be done that we cannot accomplish, thanks to the deaging and rebeautifying techniques pioneered by Dr. Leovinus in this machine. Lie back and relax while we return you to the bloom of youth. Normally, our therapy would require just a few edoes, but in critical cases such as yours a little longer may be necessary. We apologize for this delay."

The next moment, the cage fixed itself over her face and the glass case filled instantly with some purple gas. Nettie was terrified for a second, but then relaxed as the perfumes began to enter her nostrils: erotic perfumes, exotic perfumes, scents she had never imagined, scents of wonder ... at the same time the feeling on her face was inexpressibly soft and kindly. She lay back and just hoped that Dan had managed to talk to the bomb.

Dan hurried back from the Engine Room to find that Nettie had disappeared. Where he'd left her there was now a glass case filled with purple gas.

"Nettie!" he cried, banging his fists on the glass, but with no effect. He looked all around the thing, but was unable to find any off switch or any way he could prize the thing off her—if indeed Nettie was in there.

After nearly fifteen minutes of futile effort, he suddenly remembered he'd need to speak to the bomb again. So he rushed back to the Engine Room as fast as he could.

Meanwhile, The Journalist was still trying to unbutton Lucy's pin-striped power suit.

"You see, we're just not used to casual sex," he was assuring her. "Blerontinian women make such a fuss about it. You know . . . they want presents and they want to be treated nice and taken out to expensive restaurants and all that sort of crap. To meet a woman like you is just great! Let's do it again!"

"You said twice and you could think straight!" objected Lucy, whose mind was focusing on what seemed to *her* more pressing problems.

"Yeah but a handjob doesn't really count. Anyway, but us Blerontinian males'll say anything when we're aroused."

"Sixty-three . . . sixty-two . . . sixty-one . . ." said the bomb.

"Hey! Bomb! Just what d'you think you're doing?" Lucy suddenly remembered what *she* was meant to be doing.

"Pardon? Sixty . . ." said the bomb.

"I said: Bomb! What the hell d'you think you're doing?"

"Don't talk to me! Don't talk to me! This is a tricky bit! Forty-nine . . . no! Fifty-nine . . . I mean eight . . . damn! damn! There I go again, losing concentration. It's all your fault! Recommencing countdown. One thousand . . ."

"And I'm aroused now," said The Journalist.

It was at that moment that Dan burst into the Engine Room. He found the alien, to whom he'd already taken an agreeably violent dislike, kneeling behind Lucy apparently rubbing himself up against her back.

Lucy shot to her feet. "Dan!" She exclaimed, "Thank God you didn't get blown up!"

"Nine hundred ninety-six . . ." said the bomb.

"Am I interrupting something?"

"Yes!" said the bomb. "Now I've got to start all over again! One thousand . . ."

Lucy could tell Dan was not in one of his better moods. "We've just discovered how to confuse the bomb!" she said.

"Talk to it," said Dan. "Yeah! Nettie found that out."

"Oh, of course *she* would have!"

"Nine hundred ninety-four . . ." continued the bomb.

"Earth sexuality seems to be very different from Blerontinian," observed The Journalist.

"Is it really?" Dan was sizing the alien up, trying to decide which bit to punch first.

"Yes," said The Journalist putting his arms round Lucy's waist. "On Blerontin, males get what we call jealous. If one male finds another male fondling his girlfriend he can even become extremely violent."

Dan had just decided on the alien's nose as the first point of contact, when Lucy managed to disengage herself from the amorous The Journalist, and ran over to Dan. "We've got to get off this spaceship as soon as possible. I suggest The, here, stay and talk to the bomb while we go and find the Captain."

"But, you don't understand . . ." began The Journalist.

Dan decided to hold back his iron fist of retribution for the moment. He would save it for another time. "I understand only too well," he replied. "We've got to make the Captain take us back to Earth *now!*" and he was off, out of the Engine Room, and racing back down the Grand Axial Canal toward the front of the ship.

"Look, it was great making love with you," Lucy said to The Journalist, who was now standing behind her and nuzzling her, "but we've got to get back to the real world! *Our real world*." And she tried to remove his hands from her blouse.

"But Blerontinian males cannot just 'turn off' like that!"

explained The Journalist. "We need multiple satisfactions before we can return to a state of equilibrium!"

Lucy had attended self-defense classes for two years, when she had just qualified for the law, and had always slightly regretted the fact that she'd never had the chance to put her skills into practice. Consequently, it was with some satisfaction that she suddenly realized this was such an opportunity. She decided to use the standard response to the amorous-alien-fondling-you-from-behind assault. It was textbook stuff. She drove her right elbow hard into his stomach.

"Oooouuph!" gasped The Journalist.

Then she twizzled half round, caught his left wrist, and threw him over her shoulder onto the Engine Room floor.

"Oooouump!" grunted The Journalist.

Lucy spoke to him firmly in her best lawyer-speak: "You stay here, and keep talking to that bomb! While I go and find the Captain!"

Then she was out of the door, racing after Dan.

"You don't understand," The Journalist called after her, "there *isn't* any Captain on this ship!" But Lucy had gone.

"Nine hundred seventy . . ." said the bomb.

"You don't know what you're doing!" yelled The Journalist. "You're going to need me!"

"Pardon?" replied the bomb.

"I wasn't talking to you!"

"Damn!" said the bomb. "Recommencing countdown. One thousand . . . nine hundred ninety-nine . . ."

17

●

By the time Lucy caught up with Dan, he'd already found his way onto the Captain's Bridge of the *Starship Titanic*.

The main feature of the Bridge was, as The Journalist had tried to point out to them, the distinct lack of anyone or anything who could in any shape or form be referred to as "Captain." In fact, there was a distinct lack—in any shape or form—of anyone at all.

"Jesus! What do we do now?" murmured Dan as Lucy clutched his arm.

Along the length of the Bridge was a row

of windows, showing the great black immensity of space and the dazzling arm of the Milky Way along which they were headed. On the console beneath the windows were various display screens, with associated controls. The first screen showed a series of random blocks falling from the top of the screen to the bottom. The second appeared to be some sort of racing track. A third was a shoot-'em-up, and the next one along was a game apparently based on the Starship itself.

"They're all video games!" Lucy felt righteously indignant. "They aren't controls at all!"

As a matter of fact, the entire Captain's Bridge was little more than a high-class amusement arcade. It had been designed specifically to keep the Captain of the *Starship Titanic* amused during the tedium of long intergalactic flights, in a spacecraft that was almost entirely automated and self-running. It was, after all, Titania–at the heart of the ship's intelligence–who was far more capable of making decisions and issuing orders than any mere living creature.

"So?" said Dan.

"So . . ." said Lucy. "I suppose we'd better find out how to fly this baby and point her Earthwards."

"*So*–what was going on between you and that . . . that thing . . ."

"He's not a 'thing'–he's just a perfectly ordinary alien and there was nothing 'going on.'"

"He had his hands on your breasts."

"No he did not!" Lucy couldn't stand Dan at moments like this. Why couldn't he give her room? Why did he try and twist everything? What mattered was them: Lucy and Dan.

"What matters is us," said Lucy, taking her cue from the previous sentence. "You and me."

"You and me and any other life-form you can get off with!" retorted Dan.

"Jesus! Dan! You are so unpleasant!"

"I'm merely stating the facts."

"Well, if you really want to know the facts: I never made love to Jurgen Zenzendorf."

"I wasn't talking about Jurgen Zenzendorf!" Trust Lucy, thought Dan, to bring up another case that she *could* defend instead of the one they were actually talking about. "I never even suspected you of going to bed with Jurgen Zenzendorf. I mean, Jurgen Zenzendorf was an asshole."

"He was not! That's typical of you to denigrate my friends just because you're unbelievably, maniacally jealous!" Lucy was firing on all cylinders. Dan beat a hasty retreat.

"OK! OK! I accept what you say about Jurgen! He was a nice guy! I liked him. I liked his moth collection. I liked his mother. Jurgen was GREAT . . ."

"Or Jimmy Clarke!"

"Ah! Now I know you're lying!"

"HOW CAN YOU SAY THAT!"

"Jimmy Clarke told me himself you'd been to bed together."

"He's a lying bastard!"

"Anyway! That was before I knew you! I don't want to talk about any of this!"

"Then why'd you start it?" Lucy was now yelling at the top of her voice. Dan found his drive to do whatever it was he'd previously felt driven to do shrivel into a limp rag of confusion. He'd actually forgotten what they had started arguing about.

"Oh, Dan!" Lucy threw her arms round him. "Why are you always so far away?"

"I'm here, Lucy!"

"But I never seem to get through to you. I love you."

"And I love you," replied Dan, and he kissed her, and she felt how far away he really was.

"Oh, Dan, let's get married," she said.

"Oh, sure. We're on an alien spaceship—God knows how many light-years from Earth and you want to organize a wedding."

"You know what I mean," she said.

"It's no good rushing these things."

"Dan, we've been living together for thirteen years! We can't ever rush anything now!"

"Let's get the hotel up and running, and then we can talk about it," said Dan sensibly.

"You *do* like the rectory?"

"Of course I do. I'm crazy about it."

"Except that it doesn't exist anymore."

"We'll get it rebuilt—Nigel got a great deal selling off Top Ten Travel. We're rich! We'll rebuild it—better than it was— and make it the best little hotel in the goddamned world."

"If we ever get back."

"If we ever get back," agreed Dan.

They looked round at the so-called Captain's Bridge with its library, its video collection, its chessboards and cards tables, its Jacuzzi, billiard tables, cinema complex, and gym, and they wondered how the hell they were ever going to find out how to control something that didn't appear to have any controls in the first place.

"Lucy," said Dan.

"Oh! Don't start again! He wasn't doing anything!"

"I wasn't talking about that," replied Dan.

"Good!" retorted Lucy. One point scored.

"You know this video game that seems to be based on the Starship itself?"

"Uh-huh?" Lucy was staring out of the windows above the console of games.

"Well, it's sort of changing."

"I know this is stupid . . ." said Lucy. "But you don't sup- pose that computer game *isn't* a computer game?"

"You mean, it might be an actual display showing those

things coming toward us?" By now, Dan was also looking out of the window. A squadron of small, clumsy-looking spacecraft were hurtling toward the Starship. Dan checked. Their movements correlated exactly to the motion of the spacecraft on the video display.

"Oh my God!" murmured Lucy. "We're being attacked!"

At that moment, The Journalist suddenly burst onto the Captain's Bridge.

"The ship's on automatic!" he panted. "But the central intelligence core is missing some of its parts. We can't control the ship unless we can locate all the missing bits of the system and get them back into place!"

"Too late!" said Lucy and nodded out of the window. The Starship was now entirely surrounded by the smaller spacecraft.

The Journalist muttered: "Holy Pangalin!"

A voice suddenly boomed over the ship's loudspeaker system: "You are surrounded. Give up at once or we open fire!"

"Quick!" yelled Dan, pushing The Journalist over to the console. "How do we give up at once?"

"I haven't the slightest idea," returned The Journalist.

"If you refuse to give up, we shall open fire in thirty innims," said the voice from the enemy space fleet.

"WE GIVE UP!" yelled Lucy, but her voice merely echoed round the Captain's Bridge.

"DO SOMETHING!" screamed Dan.

"I told you! The ship's missing essential bits! I don't know what to do!" The Journalist was flipping controls as fast as he could to little effect.

"Since you refuse to cooperate . . ." boomed the voice.

"WE'LL COOPERATE! JUST GIVE US A CHANCE!" Lucy had climbed onto the console and was waving her arms at the spaceships in a desperate attempt to attract their attention.

". . . since you refuse to cooperate you give us no choice but to open fire."

The space outside the Starship suddenly exploded in light and a terrific noise battered the mighty hull, deafening those inside. Lucy fell off the console and Dan and The Journalist both dived for the floor, where they lay trembling with their hands over their ears.

There was then a pause.

The voice boomed over the loudspeaker again: "Do you surrender?"

"YES! YES! WE SURRENDER!" screamed all three occupants of the Captain's Bridge.

"Very well! You leave us no choice!"

Another almighty din broke out around the Starship, and this time they could feel it shudder with the impact of the explosions outside. Then there was silence. The smaller spacecraft edged in a little closer.

Then the voice was booming out again. "Look! We don't want to damage the Starship, but if you refuse to cooperate you will leave us no choice."

The Journalist had by this time found a sort of microphone. He pushed a switch and bellowed into it.

"STOP! STOP! WE SURRENDER! STOP!" His voice deafened everybody on board the *Starship Titanic,* but elsewhere there was a terrible silence. Then they heard the enemy for the last time:

"We shall hold you responsible for any damage done to the Starship!"

With that a wave of the smaller spacecraft peeled off from the main fleet and swooped toward the Starship. Points of light spattered out from their guns and the sound of ripping metal shook the great Starship.

"Oh my God!" screamed Lucy.

None of them could have told you how long the attack went on for, but it seemed like several lifetimes to the three figures huddled on the Captain's Bridge. The noise, the vibration, the crashing and bucking of the giant Starship went on and on. Lucy found The Journalist had his hands on her breasts, but decided not to say anything.

When it was all over, they waited and then stood up, trembling and shaking. The first wave was returning to the main fleet; meanwhile a second wave was peeling off.

"Here they come again!" yelled Dan, and he and Lucy

ducked down once more beneath the console. But The Journalist remained standing, with a curious expression on his face.

Lucy and Dan braced themselves for the gunfire . . . but it didn't come. Instead there was an odd, rather unmartial, banging on the hull of the ship.

"Yassaccans!" muttered The Journalist. Lucy and Dan both assumed this was another alien expletive, and remained undercover, but then The Journalist nudged Dan and said: "Look!"

Dan cautiously put his head above the console and peered out of the window: the second wave of spaceships had pulled up all around the Starship, and an army of short and stocky spacesuited figures were swarming over the hull, hammering and welding as they went.

"What the blazes?" asked Dan.

"They're repairing the damage," explained The Journalist. "Yassaccans are like that! They hate injuring hardware!"

"What about software?" asked Lucy, readjusting her bra.

"We'll need guns!" yelled The Journalist. "Follow me!" The three of them ran, doubled-up, out of the Captain's Bridge, while the enemy's hammering and welding outside gathered in intensity.

Meanwhile the voice boomed out over the loudspeakers again: "We shall recommence our attack, as soon as the first damage has been repaired! If you do not surrender, we shall board and dispose of everyone we find!"

In the crew's quarters, The Journalist discovered an arms cache. He handed out weapons to Dan and Lucy.

"How do we use them?" asked Dan, turning the strange gun over in his hand. It had a short thingy and bulbous side thingies and a sort of thingy that stuck out and which Dan pushed: a laser beam shot out across the room and exploded in a fireball at the other end.

"Like that," explained The Journalist, "except don't point them at the soft furnishings." He rushed over to the flaming curtain that Dan had just set on fire and grabbed an extinguisher.

"We can't use these!" cried Lucy.

"Then you'll just have to get used to the idea of being thrown off the ship into deep space. These Yassaccans are not playing games. Here! Dan! Put this on!" He threw Dan a helmet.

"What is it?" asked Dan.

"The Starship has two realities: one is the DataSide and the other is the MatterSide. When the Yassaccans board, they'll try to take over the DataSide as well as the MatterSide. So one of us better be prepared to confront them there!"

"I have no clue what you're talking about," replied Dan.

"It's a VR helmet—a virtual reality helmet. You put it on, you'll be able to explore the DataSide and check whatever the Yassaccans get up to there!" The Journalist was clearly losing patience.

"Just put it on!" shouted Lucy.

The noise from the repairs on the hull was getting unbearable.

"What the heck are they doing out there?" exclaimed Dan.

"Just put on the helmet!" cried Lucy. At which Dan did.

"Wow!" he exclaimed. "I see what you mean! I'm right in the ship . . . Hey! This is great! I can get into the consoles! Wow! Now I'm running along the wiring! Hey! The circuit boards are like vast cities! Shit!"

The moment Dan had the helmet on, The Journalist grabbed Lucy and started kissing her as if there were no tomorrow—which, he figured, might well be the case. And, as if she'd been expecting this all along, Lucy started to kiss him back, but then she suddenly pulled away, and glanced anxiously over at Dan, who was climbing some invisible stairs in his virtual reality and then turning around and handling invisible objects and letting out delighted yelps.

"Oh, don't worry about him!" panted The Journalist. "He can't hear or see us. We're still MatterSide. He'll be totally absorbed in that thing—it's always the same—first time you put on one of those you're usually off for five or six hours! Let's do it!"

But still Lucy pushed him away. "The Yassaccans are invading the ship!" she protested.

"That's right!" replied The Journalist. "We've hardly got time to do it before they arrive! Quick!"

"Is that all you can think about!?" groaned Lucy. The Journalist was now nuzzling her neck and sending excited shivers down her spine.

"I told you, once we Blerontinian males get aroused . . ."

"Arrgh!" Lucy suddenly screamed. "And what about the bomb?!"

"Pangalin!" exclaimed The Journalist. "I'd forgotten about that!" He suddenly whipped a small handset out of one of his many pockets and flipped it on.

"Twenty-five . . . twenty-four . . . twenty-three . . ." the bomb was counting.

"Toothless rabbits!" yelled The Journalist, "it's nearly there!"

"Twenty-two . . ." said the bomb.

"Hey! Bomb!" yelled The Journalist into the phone.

"Don't talk to me!" moaned the bomb. "I'm nearly there . . . twenty-three . . . no, I've done that . . ."

"We're being invaded!" shouted The Journalist.

"Twenty-oh . . . no! Damn! Recommencing countdown. One thousand . . ."

The Journalist flipped the phone off and started kissing Lucy's neck and undoing her suit. "That was close!" he breathed.

"Whoops! Nearly went down a transistor then!" said Dan. And suddenly Lucy was running her hands all over The Journalist and pulling him down onto the floor.

"You're crazy!" she murmured.

The hammering and banging on the outside of the ship had stopped by the time Lucy and The Journalist had struggled back into their clothes. Dan, who was still scrambling around some unseen obstacles on the DataSide, suddenly yelled out: "They're in the ship!"

The Journalist grabbed as many weapons as he could carry and headed out of the crew room. Down at the far end of the Grand Axial Canal he could see short, stocky figures already slipping onto the jetty. The Journalist settled himself behind a large podium on which one of the braziers burned, and took aim. As Lucy joined him, he fired and a series of explosions rocked the jetty and sent the invaders diving for cover.

The next moment, Lucy felt the air around and above her exploding with light and noise as the Yassaccans returned their fire.

"Hey! This air duct goes on forever!" Lucy spun round to see that Dan (still in the VR helmet and totally unconscious of anything that was happening MatterSide) had wandered out through the open door of the crew room and was now heading straight for the Grand Axial Canal.

"DAN!" she screamed, and ran toward him as his feet reached the edge of the embankment. Immediately there was another explosion of noise and light around them, as the Yassaccans fired again. But Lucy had hold of Dan's sleeve.

She managed to twist him around on the very edge of the water and pushed him back toward the crew room. The Journalist, meanwhile, was firing as fast as he could in the general direction of the invaders. But by now there was so much smoke neither side could see very much.

"Let's get out of here!" yelled The Journalist, and he bundled Lucy after Dan, back into the crew room.

18

●

"Who set fire to the curtains?" demanded Bolfass the moment he burst into the crew room. He nodded, and a couple of Yassaccan repair workers hurried over to replace them. Bolfass had led his Special Assault Group along a back service corridor to the crew's quarters, while Yellin and Assmal led the frontal attack along the main arteries of the Starship.

Bolfass loved the finish they had obtained on the service corridor ceiling. It gave him much quiet satisfaction, in the dark of night, to reflect on the craftsmanship and the high quality of material lavished on even the working areas of the great Starship.

"Never was there another such construction in the entire history of our people," he used to tell his grandchildren, as they sat around the evening hearth, eating their dumpling stew and snork crackling. "Even the curtains in the crew rooms were woven from the hair of the silky canadil, which lives high up in the Mountains of Merlor, and can only be caught with love and kindness. The hair of the canadil is so fine you must weave it by the light of the moons, for in sunlight it will disappear like snow." The children loved these tales of craftsmanship and daring feats of engineering.

It cut Bolfass to the quick to see how someone could mistreat such workmanship. In fact, it made him *very* cross indeed.

At that very moment, a figure wearing a VR helmet, stumbled into the room, followed by two others—one of whom was clearly a treacherous Blerontinian. A black rage swallowed Bolfass whole, and the next moment he had swiveled out his SD handgun and blasted the three newcomers to cosmic dust—their bodies exploded in a supernova of entrails and mangled flesh that quickly reached white-heat and, happily, burned out before they could besmatter or stain the beautifully hand-laquered walls.

Lucy was aware of a violent cacophony of noise and her eyes were whited-out by the most piercing light. She screamed, grabbed onto The Journalist, and fell in a faint upon the floor. It was that terrifying.

Bolfass grinned and blew away the smoke from his SD handgun. His anger assuaged, he twirled the gun on his finger and slipped it back into its holster.

It has to be explained at this point that the Yassaccans were a peace-loving, kindly race—dedicated to craftsmanship and sober industry. Many of them, however, were also prone to blind, blood-lusting rage when confronted by certain things, such as sloppy workmanship or a disregard for fine handcrafting. In the distant past these rages had led to terrible destruction of life and property, and since the moods went as quickly as they came, they had also led to unendurable remorse for many thousands of these otherwise benign and caring folk. The Yassaccan scientists had, therefore, developed the SD weapon, which, unlike the sort of hardware most military scientists come up with, was designed to *reduce* death and destruction rather than increase it. The Simulated Destruction weapon—or SD gun—gave the user the momentary impression of having wreaked the bloody revenge that his crazed fury craved without actually doing any damage. It always surprised and stunned the enemy, but that was all.

Lucy, not knowing any of this, was more than astonished to find herself still alive enough to hear the leader of the invaders demand: "You are under arrest! Where are the others?"

"Hey! This is great! I'm going down one of the cyber-nautic neural pathways! It's like a water slide! Wheeee! Excellent!" exclaimed Dan.

"Take that stupid thing off his head!" snapped Bolfass. The Yassaccans had no time for virtual reality exercises. Their business was exclusively MatterSide. Two of the invaders grabbed Dan and yanked the helmet off his head.

"Hey! I was enjoying th–! Jeepers! What's going on?!" said Dan as he experienced SRM–Sudden Return to MatterSide.

"I said: Where are the others?" repeated Bolfass.

"There aren't any others," replied The Journalist, truculently.

"Come on! I wasn't brought up in a Blerontinian State Nursery!* Who's running this ship?" Bolfass was getting irritated again; he'd just noticed the wretched finish on the mess tables: the Blerontinian furniture makers had used unseasoned Lintin Pine from Northern Blerontin–an inferior wood that would warp badly after a couple of decades in use . . . and . . . by the Falls of Faknik! They hadn't even concealed the end grain with housed joints! In fact, when he looked closer, he could see the tenons were barely haunched, leaving scarcely enough timber at the top of the stile for wedging! Had these people never learned even the most

---

*These institutions were infamous for turning out individuals of less than average mental agility–possibly owing to the fact that, for generations, Blerontinian governments had saved money on these establishments by forbidding any teaching to be done in them.

rudimentary basics of the art of joinery? Bolfass reached for his SD gun . . .

But before he could wreak his terrible and destructive revenge on the perpetrators of this slipshod botch-work a miracle happened.

The door of the crew room opened and a vision entered—someone so compellingly and so unutterably beautiful that Bolfass fell heavily and permanently in love. His life was never to be the same from that moment on.

He lowered the SD gun and stared in childlike adoration.

Nettie, who had just completed her course of rejuvenation in Leovinus's extraordinary beauty parlor, had not only regained her youthful complexion, but her body also had returned to its former proportions—in fact, if anything, her waist was just that little bit thinner, her breasts just a tiny bit firmer, the swell of her stomach just a tad more rounded. She looked more lovely than ever, for, despite the fresh bloom of youth that had returned to her cheeks, her face was also suffused with the wisdom that comes of having lived for several million light-years. Old Leovinus certainly knew what he was doing.

"Nettie!" murmured Dan.

"Who d'you say?" asked Bolfass absentmindedly.

"Hi! Everybody!" said Nettie. "Supposing we all introduce ourselves? I'm Nettie."

"Captain Bolfass at your service!" said Bolfass, springing to attention. "And these are Corporals Yarktak, Edembop,

Raguliten, Desembo, Luntparger, Forzab, Kakit, Zimwiddy, Duterprat, Kazitinker-Rigipitil, Purzenhakkken, Roofcleetop, Spanglowiddin, Buke-Hammadorf, Bunzlywotter, Brudel-hampon, Harzimwodl, Unctimpoter, Golholiwol, Dinsey-newt, Tidoloft, Cossimiwip, Onecrocodil, Erklehammerdrat, Inchbewigglit, Samiliftodft, Buke-Willinujit (he's a half cousin by marriage of Buke-Hammadorf) . . ."

"Hi, Nettie!" said one of the Yassaccan invaders.

"Barnzipewt," continued Bolfass, "Spighalliwiller, Mem-siportim, Itkip, Harlorfreytor, Pullijit, Beakelmemsdork, Uppelsaftat, Bukhumster, Rintineagelbun, Bootintuk, Poo-dalasvan, Sumpcreetorkattelburt . . ."

"Look! I hate to interrupt," interrupted The Journalist, "but there's a bomb on board this ship which is about to go off in . . ." He switched on the mobile phone.

"Ten . . . nine . . ." counted the bomb.

"Hot Pangalin!" exclaimed The Journalist.

"Silence! Blerontinian Purveyor of Shoddy Goods!" shouted Bolfass, grabbing the mobile phone.

"He's not a Purveyor of Shoddy Goods!" exclaimed Lucy (who, if the truth were told, was a bit hacked-off by the reaction to Nettie's entrance).

"Eight . . ." said the bomb.

"Give me that!" screamed The Journalist, flinging him-self at the phone. Bolfass tossed it to Corporal Inchbewigglit.

"Seven . . ." counted the bomb.

"It's down to seven!" yelled The Journalist.

"Take this Blerontinian Bodger to the cells!" commanded Bolfass, and Corporals Spanglowiddin and Rintineagelbun grabbed The Journalist in a half-nelson and marched him out of the crew room.

"Six . . ." said the bomb, and Corporal Inchbewigglit flicked the mobile phone off.

"These two as well!" Bolfass was pointing at Lucy and Dan.

"No!" cried Lucy and Dan. "The bomb!" but they were hustled out.

"Captain Bolfass," said Nettie in a cool voice. "There is no time to explain. Please give me the phone."

"I am afraid I cannot allow you to use it, Nettie," said Captain Bolfass, "for security reasons."

"Such as?"

"You might call for reinforcements."

"Captain Bolfass, you have my word that there is no one else on this ship, as far as I know. You also have my word that there is a bomb about to blow us all to cosmic dust, unless you give me that phone."

Bolfass hesitated a fraction of a second, and then nodded to Corporal Inchbewigglit. Corporal Inchbewigglit hesitated even less than a fraction of a second and handed the phone to Nettie. Nettie switched it on.

"Two . . ." said the bomb.

"Oh, bomb!" said Nettie. "This is Nettie. Remember me?"

"Er . . . One . . ." said the bomb.

"How fours make eight?"

"Er . . . er . . . Zeee . . ."

"*No* . . . How many *fours* make *eight*?"

"Er . . . er . . . two?" said the bomb.

"How many twos in six?"

"Three . . ." said the bomb.

"And how many times does three go into twelve?"

"Four . . ." said the bomb. It paused for a moment and then continued: "Five . . . six . . . seven . . ."

"Phew!" said Nettie. "That'll buy a bit of time . . ."

"Why have you put this bomb onto our ship?" demanded Bolfass.

"*Your* ship?" exclaimed Nettie.

"Why do you sound so surprised?" cried Bolfass. "Do you think we're not smart enough to have built such a wonderful thing?"

"Oh no!" replied Nettie. "I didn't mean anything like that; it's just that you attacked the ship. It didn't *seem* like you owned it."

"Of course we own it!" Nettie thought Captain Bolfass appeared a trifle defensive. "Legally and morally! This ship is our rightful recompense for all the misery and hardship that we have suffered at the hands of the Blerontinians!"

"Look! I don't want to appear stupid . . ."

"You could never look *that*, Nettie," the Captain assured her.

"Thank you . . ." Nettie felt herself charmed by this short, fair stranger, in whose hands her fate apparently lay. "But I don't know the background history to all this."

"And I would be delighted to tell you the whole story, dear lady"—Bolfass gave her a deep bow—"but first it is my unpleasant task to ask you once again: Why have you placed a bomb on this ship?"

"We haven't!" Nettie gave a little laugh that sent the Captain's heart reeling after his wobbly knees. "We're on this ship by accident . . ." and she told Bolfass the whole story: how Dan and Lucy were about to turn the old rectory into a hotel with the money from the Top Ten Travel Agency, and how the Starship had crashed into the house; how they had been invited aboard by a polite robot, and of all the things that had passed on the ship up until the invasion by the good Captain's forces.

When she had finished there was a long pause, until Nettie eventually added: "And that's it . . . really."

Bolfass seemed to suddenly recollect himself, as if he'd been in a dream while she'd been talking. He jumped to attention, and clicked his heels in a most courteous manner.

"I understand perfectly, dear lady," he said, bowing and kissing her hand. Captain Bolfass increasingly looked as if he had just stepped out of a Jane Austen novel.

"All we want to do is to get back to Earth," said Nettie.

"Of course!" Captain Bolfass clicked his heels again, in that way that made Nettie wriggle inside with delight. "I am entirely at your service. Come!"

And Nettie followed the Captain, her high heels clicking on the beautifully laid floor of the work area.

19

—

Dan wasn't quite sure why he was surprised to find that there were cells on the *Starship Titanic*. It made sense in a way, he supposed, and yet they seemed totally out of place amid all this luxury and elegance. The cell that he and The Journalist had been thrown into was, as cells tend to be, bare and cold. It was also damp, which is certainly what you expect cells to be but a bit surprising on such a technologically advanced vehicle.

"Lucy is such a good fuck!" said The

Journalist shaking his head in admiration. "You are a lucky man!"

"Look," said Dan, "I hate to disabuse you, but on Earth our attitude to these sorts of things is not the same as you Blerontinians. . . ."

"You're telling me!" exclaimed The Journalist. "When Lucy first suggested we have sex I could hardly believe my ears!"

"She did what?" exclaimed Dan.

"Well, we thought the bomb was going to explode any second and she just kind of . . . Hey! Come to think of it! D'you think your other friend—what's her name?"

"She *suggested* . . . you make love?"

"The blonde one—Nightie!"

"Nettie."

"D'you think Nettie knows about talking to the bomb?"

"I don't believe Lucy 'suggested you make love'!" replied Dan.

"That was when I first realized how different sexual attitudes must be on your planet!"

Dan went a bit quiet. In all the years he had known Lucy, and what was it? Oh! it must be all of thirteen years now (probably more since they'd been traveling at the speed of light!) and in all those years he couldn't remember Lucy initiating a single sexual act. In the early years, he would sometimes lie awake at night, waiting to see if she would start, but he finally gave up. She was always perfectly happy to make love—but he had to make the first approach. He'd always assumed that was just how she was.

"Hey! Jailer!" The Journalist was yelling out of the bars.

"The! Is that you?" Lucy's voice came from a cell down the row.

"Lucy!" cried The Journalist. "Pipes of Pangalin! I want to screw the arse off you!"

"STOP IT!" screamed Dan, and he threw himself at The Journalist. The two of them rolled around the sodden floor of their cell, with Dan punching and kicking and The (surprised) Journalist trying to defend himself.

"Dan! DAN! Is that you?" Lucy was yelling. She could hear them fighting. "Stop that! We've got to save our strength! We've got to get out of here!"

"Lucy's right!" The Journalist panted, and suddenly the fight went out of Dan and he found himself wondering why he was so jealous?

"Why did you attack me?" asked The Journalist.

Dan was just about to explain about the history of sexual mores on Earth, but he stopped himself. "Look!" he said instead. "Let's call a truce. Just don't talk about sex for the rest of the day, all right?"

"If you'd rather . . . But don't worry about me. I'm not shocked by the laxity of your Earth morals . . ."

"Just shut up about it for a few minutes!"

"OK!" replied The Journalist.

"Now," said Dan. "Suppose you tell me everything you

know about this starship that we're all stuck on, and then maybe together we can figure a way to get off it."

"Dan! I love you!" shouted Lucy from her cell.

"I love you, too!" Dan shouted back.

"Me too!" shouted The Journalist.

Dan fought back the urge to hit him and said: "Tell me what you know."

And so The Journalist told Dan about how the construction of the *Starship Titanic* had bankrupted the planet of Yassacca, and how Star-Struct, Inc., had then removed the construction work, without paying their debts. He told Dan of the rumors of financial trouble that had dogged the building of the ship on Blerontin, of the suspected shoddy workmanship of the Unmarried Teenage Mothers employed on the work, and how corners had been cut. He told Dan of Leovinus, the architect, engineer, artist, composer, and greatest general all-round genius in the Galaxy, and how he had met him on the night before the launch. He told Dan of his meeting with Scraliontis, the accountant, who had told him of the bomb and the plot to scuttle the great Starship and claim the insurance, shortly before plunging to his death after being attacked by a parrot.

The Journalist then told Dan how, despite his wounds, he had decided to stow away on board in order to get the great scoop that had always hitherto eluded him in his career as a journalist: he'd expose the full story behind the construction of the Starship and, at the same time, give a firsthand account of what it was like to be the only passenger on board. (The idea had been to launch the ship on automatic, before flying her to Dormillion, where she was to pick up her first crew and passengers.)

The Journalist then told Dan about how the ship had suffered a SMEF (Spontaneous Massive Existence Failure) shortly after launch and how it had crash-landed on some unknown planet in the unexplored backside of the Galaxy. He finally described how, after the crash, he had heard cries coming from one of the curtains in the First Class Dining Room. He had then discovered Leovinus where he had been left for dead by Scraliontis; The Journalist had freed him and then tried to stop the old man from rushing off the ship—but to no avail. Despite his age, Leovinus had overpowered him (The Journalist was still losing blood at this stage) and—screaming for revenge, waving a glowing silver shard in his hand, and, presumably, imagining he was still on Blerontin—the great genius had disappeared into the darkness of an alien world . . .

"Captain Bolfass wants to see you," their jailer suddenly cut across the long story. He jangled his keys as he opened the door to the wretched cell, and pulled The Journalist out.

Captain Bolfass had escorted the beautiful Nettie to the Captain's Bridge. There he had invited her to take a little tea and some cinnamon biscuits, while he made the necessary arrangements to fly the great Starship back to the planet Earth.

"Without wishing to sound disrespectful," he explained to her, "it is not a planet with which I am familiar—though, of course, it must be the most delightful world, to be the home of someone as lovely and as charming as yourself." He bowed, and Nettie felt the thrill of being treated like the heroine of *Northanger Abbey*.

"I am sure you are more than capable of guiding us home," she said, lowering her eyes.

"Ah! My dear lady!" exclaimed the Captain. "It is not *I* who will guide us but the ship itself. The exact location of the planet Earth will have been recorded in the Starship's central intelligence core. Although none of us have any idea of where your planet is to be found, all I have to do is to tell Titania—that is what Leovinus named his cybernautic system—and she will relocate it and take us there."

Captain Bolfass pressed a small button on one of the consoles, next to a video game based on a recent Blerontinian film . . . and that is where the novel suddenly ceased to be one by Jane Austen or even Catherine Cookson.

"Barthfarthinghasts!" exclaimed Bolfass. "Something's wrong! I'm getting no response!"

Nettie, who had felt Earth and home to be very close indeed—a mere button-push away—now saw it suddenly recede into deep space.

"Captain Bolfass!" Corporal Buke-Willinujit (the cousin

by marriage of Corporal Buke-Hammadorf) had just arrived out of breath and nervous. "The central intelligence core! Someone's removed the vital functions!"

Bolfass turned to Yellin, who was busy with one of the shoot-'em-up games. "This is the work of that Blerontinian Vandal! Bring him up at once!"

By the time The Journalist was thrown at his feet, Bolfass had become quite angry—not as angry as he'd have been if he had known about the substandard materials used for the railing around the Central Well, or if he had known about the scandalous lack of finish in the bilge and rubbish-disposal wastes (where the Unmarried Teenage Mothers had been told not to rub down or even apply any varnish!), but still pretty angry.

"What have you done to Titania's brain?" he roared.

The Journalist stuck his chin out and said: "I can only give you my name, rank, and number."

"This isn't *The Great Escape!*"* exclaimed Bolfass, swiveling a light into The Journalist's eyes. "Tell me what you know! Or I shall let Horst here do his worst!"

"My lips are sealed!" countered The Journalist, turning his head away.

"Very well! You leave me no choice!" snarled Bolfass and he struck The Journalist across the face with his leather glove.

The Great Escape is the name of a famous Blerontin film celebrating the true story of how the cream of the Blerontinian space fleet, held prisoners in the supposedly impregnable fortress of Drat-Kroner, contrived a mass escape. Oddly enough, it also starred Steve McQueen.

"All right!" said The Journalist. "I'll tell you anything you want! Anything!"

"Don't you want to be tortured a little more first?"

"No! I'd rather tell you now."

"Very well! We know you've sabotaged Titania's brain to prevent us from returning to Yassacca! Tell us what you've done with the parts!"

The Journalist looked surprised. "Scraliontis didn't tell me about that part of the plot!"

"What plot?" Bolfass secretly admired his Blerontinian adversary for his ability to remain cool under circumstances when a lesser man would have cracked. "It's a pity we aren't fighting this war on the same side," he thought. "On the other hand, we're not actually fighting a war at all." Bolfass made an effort to pull himself together.

The Journalist then told everything he knew about Scraliontis's and Brobostigon's plot to scuttle the great Starship and claim the insurance. Bolfass listened in white-faced anger. Nettie could see the rage boiling up within him.

Bolfass hesitated—his hand was already on his SD gun—but something in the tone of Nettie's voice stilled the fury inside him. He left his gun alone.

"They were on the ship the night before the launch," said The Journalist. "They wouldn't have wanted to attract attention by going in and out of it, so I imagine whatever they took out of the central intelligence system, they'll have hidden somewhere on board."

"Sounds feasible," said Assmal, the other Yassaccan commander, who up to this point had been doing fantastically well at the Tetrus game.

"Very well!" said Bolfass. "We will search the ship from prow to keel. Those parts must be found or we will never get Nettie back to her own planet. Indeed, we will find it hard enough to limp back to Yassacca as it is!"

"I think we can make it, Captain!" said Rodden, the navigational engineer. "We are in the Starius Zone E-D 3278 of the Praxima-Betril Section of the Inner Galaxy. I can get us home by dead reckoning, so long as Assmal can get manual control of the ship's power."

Assmal nodded. "I have control now of enough functions to be able to steer. But it will be a long trip—several hours at least."

And so, the great *Starship Titanic* turned its vast bulk in the star-bright darkness of space and began its weary journey back to the planet of Yassacca.

20

The search for the missing parts of the Starship's brain proved more difficult than anyone could have anticipated. This was mainly owing to the fact that the ship's robots were becoming increasingly eccentric in their behavior. The Doorbots were beginning to hallucinate—opening the doors for nonexistent First Class Passengers' pets and being charming to waste-disposal units. The Liftbots had gone into a permanent decline, convinced that the only way to avoid the end of civilization as they knew it was to eat less protein. The Dustbots kept dashing out from the skirting and depositing on the floor bits of fluff large enough to trip everyone up.

But the biggest problem was in the main bar of the ship, where the Barbot was trapped into some strange cyberpsychotic loop, despite the fact that they could all clearly see a piece of Titania's brain among the colored glasses and bottles on the shelf behind him.

"Yes yes sir! Jiff be with you . . . Cock this tail mix, have you just, sir . . ." The Barbot veered between the charmingly incomprehensible and belligerently drunk.

"Just give us that piece of cyberware on the shelf there . . ." tried Corporal Golholiwol. But the Barbot simply bit his nose. "Ow!" cried Corporal Golholiwol.

Every attempt to climb over the bar to get at the object was met with a surprising show of force from the Barbot, and the Peace-loving Yassaccans were forced into retreat.

By the time all but one of the missing parts were eventually located, the *Starship Titanic* was within sight of the planet Yassacca.

Returning home was always the Jailer's favorite thing in life. Soon he would have his feet up beside a blazing hearth. A jug of Old-Fashioned Beer would be in his hand, and his family would be running here and there preparing the evening meal or playing games on the porch in the setting sun.

He was therefore whistling a rather jolly tune as he

unlocked the cell door and indicated to Dan that he was a free man.

Had Dan been more musical, he would have recognized the Jailer's tune as none other than "Madamoiselle from Armentiers"—a French tune popular during the First World War. The reason why the Jailer came to be whistling it is not unconnected to the smuggling of French champagne to Blerontin via the time warp previously mentioned. For, if the truth were known, the Jailer was none other than Corporal Pilliwiddlipillipitit, the notorious smuggler and leader of the infamous Pilliwiddlipillipitit Gang, which was one of the unpleasant manifestations of organized crime that had sprung up since the ruin of the Yassaccan economy. Pilliwiddlipillipitit had disguised himself as an ordinary corporal in the Yassaccan space fleet in order to reconnoiter the *Starship Titanic* for possible plunder at a later date. But that is another story.

The moment he was free, Dan made a beeline for Lucy, who was standing on the Captain's Bridge with The Journalist and Nettie, watching the great globe of the approaching planet, through the window.

"Lucy!" he whispered. "Can we go and talk somewhere private."

"Not now!" Lucy whispered back. "Look! Isn't that the most amazing sight you've ever seen?"

"It reminds me of your breasts," murmured The Journalist. Dan managed to hold himself back, and instead of killing The Journalist on the spot, he grabbed Lucy by the arm and dragged her to the other end of the Bridge.

"You suggested it! He said you did!" Dan was trying to sound more indignant and accusing than plaintive, but it was coming out more like a total and utter whine.

"Dan! It was just a weak moment . . ."

"Why have you never had any 'weak moments' with me? In the thirteen years . . ."

"Just what the hell are you talking about, Dan? We have a great sex life, don't we?" Lucy was getting mad at him.

"Well . . . yes . . . It's just . . ."

"You're just so goddamned jealous! You think I'm chasing after every man who finds me attractive!"

"I never said that!" As usual, Dan could feel the conversation spiraling out of his control. As it happened, however, he was rescued from the ritual dialectical humiliation by a remarkable and dangerous turn of events that was to alter the whole course of this story.

Bolfass had been pointing out the continents and countries of Yassacca to Nettie. He felt his heart beating fast—partly with the pride he felt in his own world but more because Nettie had taken hold of his arm and was gazing out beside him in wonder and admiration. Bolfass could have practically swooned on the spot. He could smell the scent of that beautiful creature beside him, he could feel the gentle touch of her soft hands upon his arm, and he could feel her heart beating behind him. Bolfass hardly knew what he was saying.

"And there, dear lady, you can see the Ocean of Summer-Plastering. That is the land known as Finepottery, oh! And over there, dear lady, if you were to turn your eyes you can see my own country: Carpenters Islands. It is a fine place, peopled by noble craftsmen and technicians of the highest caliber. Or at least ... it was before ..." Bolfass's voice seemed to crack so that Nettie glanced down at him—his rugged features were clouded by a furrow of sadness.

"Before what, Captain Bolfass?" Nettie asked softly.

"Ah, Nettie, I don't want to burden you with the problems of our world," replied the gallant Captain.

"I should like to know." Nettie took the Captain's hand in hers and stroked it gently, and I think the good Captain would have fainted then and there for sheer pleasure had not a movement around the perimeter of the planet distracted him.

"Rodden! What's that?" Bolfass had suddenly become tense.

The Navigational Engineer peered into the distant haze around Yassacca. He put his binofocals to his eyes and an involuntary gasp escaped him.

"Blerontinians!" he murmured.

Bolfass grabbed the binofocals. Yes! He could clearly see a whole fleet of fighter spaceships with Blerontinian registration plates, but no other markings. They were clearly not the official Blerontin Space Fleet.

"Mercenaries!" muttered Assmal.

"They mean trouble!" said Yellin.

"Quick!" yelled Bolfass. "Every man to arms! And turn off the SD feature. We shall shoot real ammunition!"

There was a buzz among the Yassaccans as they leapt into action, grabbing weapons and racing to predetermined positions. The idea of firing real ammunition instead of Simulated Destruction charges was both terrible and exciting. It was one thing to use live ammunition against the outside hull of the Starship, but shooting live rounds actually *inside* the ship would mean damage on a grand scale! There would be an enormous amount of exciting repair work to look forward to!

Bolfass's face suddenly darkened, and he turned gravely to Nettie. "Nettie!" he said. "I am so sorry to do this, and I hope you will be able to forgive me, but I must regretfully ask you and your friends to retire to a safe quarter while we are engaged with the enemy."

While Bolfass had been saying this, the Blerontinian mercenaries had streaked (at just under light-speed) up to the Starship, and had now surrounded it. There must have been fifty or sixty craft—a typical ragbag assortment of spaceships converted to military use. Such ad-hoc fleets had become a familiar sight in the space-skies around this sector of the

Galaxy, ever since the breakdown of economic cooperation between worlds and the destabilization of the Intergalactic Security Council.

Suddenly a harsh voice boomed out over the Starship's loudspeaker system: "This is the official space fleet of the Magna-Corps Insurance Company of Blerontin. We are acting under license and according to Blerontinian Law on behalf of the Loss Adjusters appointed to liquidate the remaining assets of the Star-Struct Construction Company, Starship Titanic Holdings, Ltd., and Starlight Travel, Inc., as per the insurance schedule para- six, subsection three. On behalf of the above-named Insurance Company, we hereby repossess this starship as lawful property of the said Insurance Company. Please leave quietly and in an orderly fashion."

"Snork Piddlers!" yelled Bolfass. He knew how to work the ship's communication systems, and his voice rang round the mercenaries' spacecraft so loudly they could hear it from the Starship! "We built this ship! We lavished our care and craftsmanship on it without stint and without grudge! We bought the finest materials and ran into debt trying to meet the wonderfully high specifications ordered by Mr. Leovinus. We were never paid a penny. Then, when the construction was taken from us, we and our families were faced with poverty and hunger. This ship is ours by every moral right in the Galaxy. What is more, we claim it by right of salvage! We found it, and we have brought it back to its rightful place! Go suck yourselves!"

Even as he spoke, four of the mercenary boarding craft clanged into the side of the Starship. Grappling irons were attached to the hull and the air locks of the *Titanic* were broached from the outside.

At the same moment, the air around the mercenaries burst into light and smoke and noise, as the Yassaccans launched a furious counterattack.

All this while, Nettie, Dan, Lucy, and The Journalist had found themselves back under arrest and being hurried toward the cells by half a dozen agitated Yassaccan guards. They were about halfway along the Grand Axial Canal when an advance patrol of Blerontinian mercenaries suddenly burst out of the Embarkation Lobby and opened fire. The three Earth people and The Journalist threw themselves onto the floor, but the Yassaccans, used as they were to SD weapons, hesitated for a second and in that second they lost it. Corporals Inchbewigglit and Kazitinker-Rigipitil made it to the deck but Corporals Yarktak, Bunzlywotter, Tidoloft, and Forzab received direct hits. They clutched their chests and their weapons clattered to the floor.

Nettie was the first to throw herself onto one of the fallen guns and without hesitation she turned it on the mercenaries. Considering she had never even handled a shotgun back on Earth, Nettie seemed to master the Yassaccan "blaster" with remarkable ease. It seemed obvious to her where to hold it, and she'd noticed the trigger just below one of the firing chambers. She aimed it and squeezed the trigger—flame blasted out of the barrels and two mercenaries fell to the ground.

"No! No!" yelled Corporal Inchbewigglit in alarm. "Aim above their heads!"

"Not on your life!" yelled Nettie, and brought down another Blerontinian. By this time Lucy, Dan, and The Journalist had each grabbed hold of another weapon and started blasting away at their attackers.

Their Yassaccan guards were clearly shocked. The Blerontinians, for their part, were taken totally by surprise. They were used to standing up to the fury of Yassaccan SD guns, and, in extreme circumstances, they were used to Yassaccans firing real weapons over their heads. But this was something new! It was also very alarming! The few Blerontinians who remained standing looked at their fallen comrades, they looked back at their adversaries, who even now were blasting straight at them. Without waiting for another volley to hit them, they turned and fled.

The Yassaccan guards were flabbergasted. Never, in the history of their nations, had Blerontinians fled before Yassaccan gunfire!

Nettie, meanwhile, had raced to the doors of the Embarkation Lobby. There she continued to blast away at the retreating Blerontinians. But the mercenaries were already back in the air lock and had slammed the door shut.

"Mind the paintwork!" gasped Corporal Inchbewigglit.

"Well done!" cried Dan, who had just reached Nettie. She was breathing hard, and Dan could feel the heat coming off her body as he stood close behind her. Suddenly she spun round.

"Oh my God! The bomb!" she exclaimed and pulled the mobile phone from her pocket.

"Two . . ." said the bomb. "One . . ."

"Hi, Bomb! It's Nettie!"

"Hi, Nettie . . ."

"Are you all right, bomb?"

There was silence. For a moment, Dan thought they'd lost it.

"Bomb? Are you there, bomb?" Nettie called into the phone. But still the bomb didn't reply.

"Bomb!" Dan had grabbed the phone.

"Oh! Of course! Let the man do it!" said Nettie.

"Bomb? Are you there?" Dan wasn't listening to Nettie. "Speak to me!"

"I was speaking to Nettie," said the bomb in a sulky voice.

"Oh," said Dan and handed the phone back to Nettie. "Sorry," he whispered.

"This is Nettie," said Nettie into the phone. Again the bomb remained silent. "Bomb?" she repeated.

Again silence.

"Bomb!" a note of urgency had crept into Nettie's voice. "Speak to me!"

Then the bomb spoke . . . very quietly . . . "I'm a Mega-Scuttler . . ." it said.

"Is that your name?" asked Nettie.

"Yes," said the bomb. "I'm a bomb."

"I know you are," replied Nettie.

"I like hearing your voice, Nettie," said the bomb.

"I like hearing yours, bomb," replied Nettie.

"You're not . . . just saying that?"

"No, I'm not. For an electronic voice, you have a very soft one. It's nice." For a moment Nettie thought the bomb was crying. "Won't you start counting down again for me?"

"If you'd really like me to," said the bomb.

"Yes," said Nettie.

"Very well," said the bomb. "I'll count—just for you, Nettie. But this is the last time . . . The very last time . . ."

Pause.

"I'm just doing this for you, Nettie."

"Thank you, bomb."

"Good luck, Nettie."

"Good luck, bomb."

"One thousand . . . nine hundred ninety-nine . . ."

Nettie had been so intent upon her purpose of stopping the bomb that she hadn't realized how terrified she'd been, but the next moment she found out: her knees gave way, and she fell into Dan's arms, which were suddenly there to catch her.

Bolfass stood on the Captain's Bridge of the *Starship Titanic* and could not believe his eyes as he watched the Blerontinian mercenaries beat a retreat into their boarding craft.

"What on Yassacca's going on?" he exclaimed. "Bleron-tinians don't just give up like that—they usually fight to our last man!" But, for good measure, he ordered another salvo of space-fire and the blackness around the mercenaries' craft exploded again with light and noise. In less time than it takes for a snork to poop on a plate, the ragtag flotilla had turned about, and with a blast of white-hot rocketry the loss adjusters' space fleet disappeared into the stars beyond the beautiful green planet of Yassacca.

At that very moment, Dan and Nettie burst onto the Captain's Bridge again.

"You should be in the cells!" snapped Bolfass.

"They shot straight at the enemy!" Corporal Inchbewigglit appeared behind them. "That's why the mercenaries ran off!"

"We've got to do something about the bomb!" cried Nettie. "It says this will be its last countdown."

"That's terrible!" exclaimed Bolfass, looking very grave indeed.

"Yes! It says it will expode this time!"

"You *aimed* directly *at* the Blerontinians?"

"Isn't that what you're meant to do?" asked Nettie.

"No it is *not*!" exclaimed Bolfass. "We have a strict moral code! My dear lady! I'm sure you didn't mean to actually aim *at* them?"

"Well, of course she did!" Dan was getting a bit short-tempered. "It was the only way to stop them. What are we going to do about the bomb?"

"They ran off like zippo as soon as they realized Nettie was firing at them!" exclaimed Inchbewigglit enthusiastically.

"I shall have to put you all under arrest!"

"Captain Bolfass," said Nettie in her most charming voice. "We are ignorant of your ways on Yassacca, and can only react as Earth people, and on Earth, I'm afraid people aim to kill and maim each other. That's what weapons are for. I don't like it, but that is how it is. We didn't mean to infringe your code of honor; we just tried to save you and the Starship from the loss adjusters. Now listen . . ." and she flipped on the mobile phone.

"Nine hundred twenty-two . . ." the bomb was still counting.

"We've got about thirteen minutes!"

"Very well," said Bolfass, still stern-faced. "We shall have to apologize to the Blerontinians."

"But they were trying to kill *you*!" exclaimed Nettie.

"That is because they have no moral code that forbids them," replied Bolfass, with undeniable logic. "I shall write the letter of apology as soon as I get a spare moment."

"If we don't do something about the bomb," exclaimed Dan, "we're all of us going to be nothing *but* spare moments!"

"You are right!" said Bolfass. "I shall have it defused at once!"

Nettie insisted on being with the bomb while it was defused. "I feel I owe it to it," she said, when Dan tried to dissuade her. "Besides, if it goes off, it doesn't matter where on the ship any of us are."

The Yassaccan bomb-disposal expert agreed, as he put his tool bag down beside the bomb.

"Four hundred thirty-four . . ." said the bomb.

"Hi, bomb!" said Nettie.

"Four hundred thirty-three . . ." said the bomb. Nettie somehow knew that it was not going to let itself be interrupted. This was the last countdown.

"How are you feeling, bomb?" Nettie asked.

"Please don't talk to it while I'm defusing it," said the bomb-disposal expert. "It could be dangerous."

"Have you got enough time?" asked Dan.

"Four hundred thirty-two . . ." said the bomb.

"Depends," said the bomb-disposal expert, unscrewing a metal plate from the cabinet. "If it keeps counting at this speed I should be OK, but sometimes on the last countdown they can speed up. This is an 8D-96 Full Force Mega-Scuttler—if it were 8G or even a 9A we'd be fine. They put a servo-control mechanism in to stop that problem. But with the 8D, well . . . you just never know . . . Ah! This seems to be all in order . . ."

While he had been talking the bomb-disposal expert had removed the metal plate and exposed a dull red button which read: DEFUSE THE BOMB

"Fortunately, on the 8D they still included this automatic defuser—just to make it simple for us bomb-disposal experts."

He pressed the button. Immediately the bomb stopped counting. There was a pause. Then a siren went off, the red button saying DEFUSE THE BOMB lit up and started flashing, and a glass cover slid across the button, preventing anyone from touching it.

"Wait a mo . . ." said the bomb-disposal expert. "This doesn't seem to be quite right . . ."

"Congratulations!" said the bomb. "You have successfully defused the 8D-96 Full Force Mega-Scuttler. The Mega-Scuttler, however, is linked into the intelligence cybersystem of this starship, and unfortunately that system is currently incomplete. The bomb has therefore gone into Default Mode. Please refer to manual."

"Where's the manual?!" asked the bomb-disposal expert—his voice betraying an edge of what Nettie (although she desperately tried to find a more comforting word) could only categorize as "panic."

"You're the bomb-disposal expert," said Dan helpfully.

Meanwhile, Nettie had discovered a small booklet tucked under the bomb cabinet. She riffled through the pages.

"How to preset the timer for cooking large joints!" she read.

"That's the manual for the gas oven!" exclaimed the bomb-disposal expert, grabbing it off Nettie and starting to read it avidly. Any technical manual was of interest to a Yassaccan. It was the sort of thing in which they could always find solace and escape, especially when under pressure.

Meanwhile Dan and Nettie were scouring the engine room for the right manual. By the time the bomb-disposal expert said: "Look! It has the self-cleaning function!" Dan had found the "Easy-to-Use Manual for the 8D-96 Full Force Mega-Scuttler, Your User-Friendly Bomb" stuffed behind some water pipes.

"The 8D-96 Full Force Mega-Scuttler is designed to be the Ultimate User-Friendly Exploding Device," he read. "All operations are simple and self-explanatory . . ."

"Give me that!" cried the bomb-disposal expert, snatching the manual from Dan's hands. "Default Mode," he read. "Once the bomb has gone into Default Mode, as a result of an incomplete intelligence system on board ship, the following conditions will apply: You will not be able to reach the defuse button. You will not be able to touch the bomb or the bomb cabinet. You will not be able to do anything anymore to the bomb. So leave it alone. D'you understand? Good. The 8D-96 Full Force Mega-Scuttler will now explode in exactly six Dormillion days from the commencement of Default Mode."

"Shit!" said Dan.

"Shit!" said Nettie.

"Shit!" said the bomb-disposal expert.

21

"How long *is* a Dormillion day?" It was Nettie who was first to ask the obvious question.

"Thirty-six Dormillion hours," said the bomb-disposal expert.

"How long's a Dormillion hour?" asked Dan.

"Seventy-eight Dormillion minutes," said the bomb-disposal expert. "It's about . . . well . . . How can I tell you? There's no point of reference."

The three of them thought for some time and were just about to agree that it was impossible to convey any idea of time from one star system to another, when Nettie said:

"Got it!"

I won't tell you how she worked it out, but it was pretty clever. If you can't work it out for yourself, you'll have to write to the publishers of this book for a self-explanatory leaflet entitled "How Nettie Worked Out the Length of a Dormillion Day."

"So . . . Six Dormillion days must be roughly equivalent to ten Earth days!" said Nettie, after a few quick calculations.

"God! Nettie!" said Dan. "You're so clever. Why didn't I think of that?"

The trio had just reported back to the Bridge of the Starship.

"How do we get it out of Default Mode?" Bolfass was questioning the bomb-disposal expert.

"Our only hope is to find the missing central core of the ship's intelligence," said the bomb-disposal expert. "If we can replace that, then I can probably defuse the bomb. Otherwise it'll blow in six Dormillion days."

Bolfass turned to his assembled crew. "Men! You hear the seriousness of this situation. Our beloved home of Yassacca has been ruined by the construction of this Starship and the failure of the Blerontinians to honor their debts. We built in good faith. We put our entire way of life at risk to construct the most fabulous and beautiful starcraft the Galaxy has ever seen. The Blerontinians betrayed our trust. The only chance our world has of returning to its former prosperity is by our repossession of the *Starship Titanic*. If it is blown up by this treacherous bomb, the future of our world is grim indeed.

"Therefore, I command you to search this ship again. I know we have scoured every last inch of it, but that missing central intelligence core must be on board somewhere, and we *must* find it . . ."

At this moment a scream was heard over the loudspeaker system.

"Lucy!" exclaimed Dan.

I have to explain what had happened to Lucy and The Journalist since the brief exchange of gunfire outside the Embarkation Lobby. The moment Nettie, Dan, and Corporal Inchbewigglit ran after the retreating Blerontinians, The Journalist grabbed Lucy and pulled her into a side chamber off the Grand Axial Canal.

"What on Earth are you doing, The!" exclaimed Lucy, although it was pretty obvious that what The Journalist was doing was undoing the buttons of her pin-striped power suit as fast as he possibly could, while at the same time apparently trying to see how far into her ear he could stick his tongue. "The!" cried Lucy. "Stop it!"

"No! No! No!" moaned The Journalist. "Once we Blerontinian males have been aroused by a female, it takes us many

many years—sometimes a lifetime—to get dearoused vis-à-vis that particular female."

"What are you saying, The?" cried Lucy.

"Marry me, Lucy!" cried The Journalist burying his face in her now exposed bra.

"Oh yes! Yes! Yes! The!" she cried.

"Squawk!" cried something else.

"We can get engaged and have a white wedding and a wedding cake and Dan can give the best man's speech and we'll have a honeymoon!" exclaimed The Journalist.

"Squawk!"

"Darling The!" cried Lucy, tears in her eyes. "What am I doing? What am I saying?" Part of Lucy's legal training had suddenly started to reassert itself. It was something along the lines of: don't commit to anything that you might later regret. "But I'm getting married to Dan! We're going to run a hotel! What was that squawk?"

"Squawk!" said the thing that was squawking.

"It was that!" exclaimed The Journalist, and suddenly a large parrot flew out of the dark recesses of the room and landed on The Journalist's shoulder. It was at that moment that Lucy screamed, and as she screamed, as luck would have it, she had inadvertently put her hand down on one of the ship's intercom buttons, with the result that her scream was relayed all round the *Starship Titanic*.

"Squawk!" said the parrot. "Bloody Genius!"

Back on the Captain's Bridge Bolfass pricked up his ears. "What did that parrot say?"

"BLOODY GENIUS!" screamed the parrot over the intercom.

"Parrot!" yelled Captain Bolfass. "What are you telling us?"

"Bloody genius!" repeated the parrot.

"PARROT!" Bolfass yelled into the intercom. "We're looking for the missing central intelligence core for Titania's brain, do you know where it is?"

There was a silence.

"PARROT!" yelled Bolfass, but Lucy had removed her hand from the intercom button and was now using it to caress The Journalist's face as if his smooth features were a fortune-teller's crystal ball.

"Why's Captain Bolfass so interested in what a parrot says?" Nettie had turned to Corporal Inchbewigglit.

"In Yassaccan tradition," whispered Corporal Inchbewigglit, "parrots are the messengers of truth. We have a saying: 'From the mouths of babes and parrots.'"

Lucy, meanwhile, was wondering why she had said yes to everything The Journalist had just suggested. She thought she had probably made a terrible mistake. If only she could see the future in those strange orange-colored eyes of his. "You're crazy!" she said.

"Ohhh!" moaned The Journalist, as he chewed her bra strap.

"Ahh!" said Lucy.

"Haaaa!" murmured The Journalist.

"Oh-uh!" replied Lucy.

"Oooooh!" he said.

"Oh! Uh! Ooh!" added Lucy.

"Ya! Ha! Haa?" asked The Journalist.

"Uh!" confirmed Lucy.

"Uh?" asked The Journalist again.

"Uh!" repeated Lucy.

"Uuuuuhh!" The Journalist was almost lost for words at this point. But Lucy carried on the conversation:

"OH!" she said.

"Ah?" he wondered how she could be so certain.

"AH!" she nodded. She was absolutely certain now. "AH!"

And at that moment the entire company from the Captain's Bridge burst into the side chamber off the Grand Axial Canal, and stood riveted to the spot while they watched a highly qualified lawyer from Wilshire Boulevard and an underachieving member of Blerontinian press corps doing the sort of things to each other that give inexpressible delight and pleasure to the participants, but which only tend to provoke ridicule from casual observers, and about which, therefore, I will not go into detail. Suffice it to say that the moment the Bridge party burst into the room, the parrot gave the loudest squawk it had given up to date, and Lucy fell off the table onto The Journalist's face.

"LUCY!" exclaimed Dan.

"Parrot!" yelled Bolfass. "Where is the missing intelligence core for Titania's brain?"

"Bloody Genius!" squawked the parrot.

"Don't talk rubbish!" shouted Bolfass.

"BLOODY GENIUS!" screamed the parrot.

"I ASKED YOU A QUESTION!" yelled Bolfass. Also according to Yassaccan tradition, parrots were supposed to answer any questions put to them.

"Squawk!" The parrot momentarily forgot its powers of speech.

"ANSWER MY QUESTION!"

"SQUAWK!"

The parrot flew off into the shadows at the farther end of the chamber.

"Damn it!" Bolfass knew it was bad luck if a parrot refused to answer your question.

"I can explain everything," Lucy was telling Dan.

"No! You can't! You can't explain ANYTHING!" screamed Dan. And Lucy suddenly thought, "He's right! . . . He's absolutely RIGHT!"

"Perhaps that *is* your answer!" It was Nettie who had suddenly stepped forward and taken Captain Bolfass by the arm.

"Dear lady, it is good of you to trouble yourself with this

matter, but I fear the parrot has not given any reply. I am doomed."

"Didn't you tell me that this Starship was designed by some genius?"

"Leovinus!" exclaimed The Journalist. "He was here on the ship when we crashed on Earth!"

"Maybe *he* has the missing part?" It was all so clear to Nettie, although she didn't know why.

Something clicked in The Journalist's mind. "Of course!" he exclaimed. "When he ran off the ship—he was brandishing this glowing silver strip in his hand . . ."

"The central core intelligence!" exclaimed Bolfass.

"That's why it isn't on the ship!"

"So . . ." Captain Bolfass was putting two and two together but rather slowly.

"In order to get the missing central intelligence core for the ship's system, we've got to find this Leovinus character." Nettie had decided to take over the deduction process. "Leovinus is on Earth. But we can't get to Earth because we don't know where it is, and the only way to find out where it is, is to get hold of the missing central intelligence core and refit it into Titania's brain. Gentlemen, we're screwed."

It was then that the docking sirens sounded. The *Starship Titanic* was preparing itself for landing on the planet of Yassacca.

22

⬮

The celebration party was a gloomy affair.

Everyone tried to make the best of it, and kept toasting the Earth folk for their invaluable help in routing the insurance loss adjusters; several speeches were made extolling the return of the great Starship to its rightful home, but nobody could forget that within a couple of days, the ship would have to be towed off to some distant part of the Galaxy, where it could explode without doing any more harm than destroy itself.

The Yassaccans could see no prospect of

recovering their economy. Meanwhile, Lucy, Dan, and Nettie could see no prospect of ever returning to their own planet. They had each been given translation blisters (like small plasters worn behind the ear) so they could still communicate now that they were away from the influence of the ship's automatic systems, but that had done little to reconcile them to the prospect of exile on an alien world.

"But surely," Rodden, the Navigational Officer, had cornered Nettie, "you must have *some* idea of where this 'Earth' place is? I mean, you must at least know whether it is in the Notional Northern Hemisphere of the Galaxy or the Notional South?"

"Well . . . no . . ."

"Is it on an outer or an inner arm of the spiral?"

"I haven't a clue," said Nettie.

Rodden shook his head gloomily. He hated talking to dumb blondes. "Well, if you really have no idea where you've come from, I really can't get you back there. The only thing that could is the Starship and that can't remember because its brain's missing! Seems to be a common complaint . . ." he added, unnecessarily, and wandered off, rather to Nettie's relief.

Nettie looked around at the gloomy party. She felt sad, and yet, there was so much beauty in this gentle world she found herself in. Yassacca! It was a nice name for a start. And she was sure there were worse places . . . Slough . . . New Malden . . . Basingstoke . . . Nettie found herself split in two.

One part of her was saying: Come on! Make the best of it! This is home from now on! And the other half was telling her not to give up . . . that somehow, deep down inside her, she was convinced that she would be able to get them all back to Earth. Nettie felt a bit foolish for feeling so convinced of her own ability, but there it was—she just couldn't shake the feeling off, though she had no idea why she had it.

In the meantime, she tried to enjoy the celebration.

The very smell of the snork roasting over open fires seemed sad, as it wafted under the gloomy Yassaccan pines and then mingled with the softer, sadder scents of the night jasmine and the weeping oleanders that crowded Corporal Golholiwol's garden. The Yassaccans took turns hosting important national events, and it just happened to be Corporal Golholiwol's turn. He had provided seven snorks for roasting, plates of fish and fruit and fresh vegetables from his garden. Unlike the Blerontinians, the Yassaccans took no interest in canapés and preferred good plain food washed down with plenty of Yassaccan ale and sweet potato wine.

The Journalist gloomily thought it all pretty poor fare, but he tried to hide his contempt for the lack of "fish-paste," tiny chicken vol-a-vents, and cocktail sausages on sticks.

But, no matter how much Nettie complimented him on his crackling, Corporal Golholiwol refused to emerge from *his* gloom. "In the old days," he explained to Nettie, "we would have roasted *seventy* snorks! I would have been able to provide so much fish we could have filled the Ocean of Summer Plastering! And all the beer and wine . . . well! It would have flowed from those fountains you see over there in the center of the garden . . . ah! These are thin times indeed for Yassacca." And he gloomily stared into the empty ale mug he held in his hands.

Captain Bolfass was also gloomy. He kept trying not to stare at Nettie, who had discarded her GAP T-shirt, hand-knitted waistcoat, and mini-skirt in favor of a simple Yassaccan shift, slit up to the thigh and embroidered at one corner. She looked breathtaking, and the poor Captain's breath was so taken that he sighed and tried to imagine how he could ever have lived without her.

"Who are you mooning over now, Captain Bolfass?" asked his wife.

"Excuse me, my dear," replied Bolfass, "it is just that young Earth woman who has stolen my soul with her beauty."

"Poor dear!" said Mrs. Bolfass, taking his hand and stroking it. "I'm sure you'll get better."

"Ah!" sighed Captain Bolfass. "I do hope so . . . I do hope so."

"Perhaps you should see Dr. Ponkaliwack?"

"No . . . no . . . I'll be all right . . ." sighed the Captain. (On Yassacca, being "in love" was considered a form of illness.)

But the old Yassaccan songs, that the band were now playing, caused the Captain to sigh again and again and even brought a tear to his eye. They were ancient songs of yearning for better tools and materials, songs of lament for construction projects that were never finished, and songs of regret for the great craftsmen of yesteryear who would never plane nor chisel again.

Lucy found Dan hidden at the far end of the garden, sitting on a low wall under the oleanders, sunk in utter despondency. He held a piece of snork crackling in one hand and a glass of wine in the other. "Go away!" he said.

"Oh, Dan!" Lucy sat beside him and tried to put her arm around him. "Let's get married!"

"Married!" exclaimed Dan. "Huh! After what I saw that alien doing to you?"

"Don't be . . ." well Lucy wasn't quite sure what she was telling Dan not to be: "foolish?" "jealous?" "sulky?" He had a right to be all those things, and yet . . . she couldn't help feeling he was overdoing it. "Dan! We love each other, don't we?"

"I don't know," replied Dan. "Do we?"

"Of course we do!" cried Lucy. "We're going to set up the hotel and run it together and have children . . ."

"No we aren't," said Dan. "We can't get back to Earth and even if we could, the hotel's a pile of rubble!"

"But we've got the money from Top Ten Travel!"

"But that doesn't mean we love each other!"

"But we do! We've been together all this time!"

Dan stared gloomily at the piece of snork crackling in

his hand. Finally he looked at Lucy and said: "Here comes Nettie."

Nettie had been looking for Lucy and Dan all over the garden. "May I join the funeral?" she said.

Dan nodded and Nettie sat down on the other side of him. Lucy took her hand away from Dan's.

"So," Nettie began. "I suppose this is going to be home from now on."

"You look as if you've made yourself pretty much at home already," remarked Lucy, who was still wearing her Earth clothes.

"I thought I might as well start getting into the role," laughed Nettie.

"That is *so* sensible," said Dan, to Lucy's intense annoyance.

"Look, I don't want to break you two up . . ." said Nettie, even more to Lucy's intense annoyance, "but I've got something to tell you . . . Something I think you ought to know . . ."

Nettie didn't quite know where to begin. "It's about the rectory . . . your hotel . . ." she said.

"It's sad to think we'll never be able to run it after all, Nettie," Dan sighed into his wine.

"You were never going to be able to run it," replied Nettie.

"What d'you mean?" Lucy was immediately on the defensive. What was Nettie implying? That they were incompetent or something?

"I don't know whether I should tell you this now . . . maybe it's pointless . . . But on the other hand, maybe it'll make you feel better . . ."

"What?" demanded Lucy. She stood up and folded her arms, in her best courtroom "how do you dare propose *that*" posture.

"Well . . ." said Nettie, "Nigel was a shit—we all know that . . ."

"He was my best friend!" exclaimed Dan.

"Yes . . . sure . . ." replied Nettie. "But he was a shit."

"You certainly let him treat *you* like shit!" retorted Lucy.

"That's my problem," replied Nettie. "I'm crazy. But that doesn't mean I'm stupid. And although Nigel never discussed any of his business with me, I can tell you he didn't sell Top Ten Travel for anything like the amount he told you he had. That's why you could never get the documentation off him. He actually sold it for peanuts. You'd never have been able to pay off the rectory—let alone set up the hotel."

There was a brief silence that seemed to get up, stretch its legs, and then wander off into the night.

"Huh!" snorted Lucy eventually. "That doesn't surprise me one little bit!"

"Well! It sure surprises me!" exclaimed Dan. "How d'you know this, Nettie?" He felt incredibly indignant—probably indignant at Nigel, but for the moment, he was content to be indignant with the messenger.

"Oh . . ." said Nettie, "he was so sloppy—he used to leave

documents just lying around. I guess he never bothered to talk to me enough to find out that I was bright enough to see what he was up to. I kept trying to tell you, but we never met except with Nigel in tow. It was awful; I could see you heading for disaster."

"That bastard!" cried Lucy, striding around beneath the oleanders. "If we ever get back to Earth I'm going to tear his balls off!"

"Well, that's one threat he doesn't have to worry about," sighed Dan, his depression deepening by the second. Suddenly he felt Nettie's hand on his arm. He turned and looked directly into her eyes and felt his stomach give way. A wave of wonderful helplessness swept over him, as he felt her eyes falling into his. And yet she was saying something else. Dan couldn't make out what it was that Nettie was saying, he was so overcome with her proximity and the way her breasts moved under the translucent muslin of her Yassaccan shift. The next moment, before he regained his senses, she had rushed off in some excitement.

Dan turned to Lucy. "What did she just say?" he managed to ask.

"She just said: 'Wait a minute! I've got it! I've got the answer! I knew I would!'" replied Lucy.

"Oh!" said Dan.

There was a silence. Then he added: "I'm sorry about the hotel. I know how much it meant to you."

Lucy looked at him in some surprise. "I was more worried for you. I know you'd staked everything on it." Dan frowned and took a little swig of his wine. "That's why I went along with it," continued Lucy. "I never really liked the rectory that much. I just couldn't bear for *you* to be disappointed."

Dan took another little swig of his wine. Then he did something that was so uncharacteristic that it made Lucy jump out of her skin: he threw his glass against one of the oleanders and it shattered into tiny pieces.

"Well," he said. "In that case, I guess we've both been fooling ourselves and each other for a long time. I was only so keen because I thought you were."

Lucy was playing with one of the buttons that had come off her pin-striped power suit during her earlier encounter with The Journalist. "Maybe that says it all, Dan . . . Maybe that says it all."

23

▬

Dan found Nettie in a state of some agitation. She had just been proposed to by Captain Bolfass, Corporal Inchbewigglit, Corporal Rintineage-lbun, Corporal Buke-Hammadorf, his half-cousin by marriage Corporal Buke-Willinujit, Buke-Willinujit's father, Corporal Golholiwol, the Yassaccan Prime Minister, and several other Yassaccans she did not actually know, on her way across the lawn. The Prime Minister had even given her a bottle of famous Yassaccan scent. "Only wear it for us Yassaccans, my dear," he had said and squeezed her bottom.

When Dan caught up with her Nettie was desperately looking for her handbag.

"God! You don't think anyone's stolen it, do you?"

"I believe they don't have much crime here on Yassacca," said Dan.

"There's been all this organized crime since the economy went down the chute," said Nettie.

"But organized crime isn't going to bother to steal your handbag, Nettie!" Dan was trying to be reassuring.

"I've got to find it!" exclaimed Nettie, her eyes were blazing just a few inches away from Dan's. Dan's knees suddenly relaxed their grip on the standing up situation, and he had to sit down on the nearest tree stump.

"Great grief! That wonderful scent you're wearing!"

"The Prime Groper of Yassacca just gave it to me . . . in more ways than one," replied Nettie.

"Nettie! I . . ." Dan didn't really have a clue what he wanted to say. It was as if the scent had wrapped itself around him and wouldn't let go until he told her the truth.

"What?" Nettie was back searching a pile of clothes that various people had dumped over a bed that was standing on the veranda of Corporal Golholiwol's house.

"Nettie I . . . I think . . . I . . . I'm crazy about you!" Dan didn't know quite how it happened, but suddenly he had his arms around Nettie's waist and was kissing the back of her neck. Nettie spun round.

"Stop that!" she cried. Dan backed off. "You're getting

married to Lucy! You're going to start a hotel! You're going to have kids and all that sort of thing!"

"Everything's changed!" said Dan. "We can't go back to Earth. It's all different here!" And he tried to put his arms around her again. But Nettie backed away.

"Now hold on, Romeo!" said Nettie. "I'm not an emotional doormat for your convenience! Besides! You're going back to Earth! We're *all* going back to Earth—I hope—just as soon as I find my handbag!"

"What have you got in your handbag? A Concorde ticket home? A pocket rocket?" Dan didn't doubt for a moment that Nettie had the solution if she said she had—he knew that if any one of them had the brains to get them back it would be Nettie. He worshiped her. He admired her. But why couldn't he tell her properly instead of behaving like a sex-crazed half-wit?

"Let's just find it, shall we?" said Nettie. So Dan stopped asking questions and put his mind to looking for the handbag.

"I'm sorry! Are you looking for this?" Corporal Golholiwol was holding up Nettie's handbag. Nettie grabbed it, opened it, and started feverishly rummaging through it.

Dan looked at Corporal Golholiwol. "Nettie's got something in it that will help us get back to Earth." He hoped Nettie wouldn't hear how like a sex-crazed half-wit he sounded.

"Would it be these?" Corporal Golholiwol held up a

package, neatly wrapped in a broad leaf. Nettie snatched it from him, checked its contents, and then looked up at the corporal.

"What the blazes do you mean by taking things out of my handbag?" Her eyes were like miniature SD guns. Corporal Golholiwol felt himself disintegrate and splatter all over the veranda. He looked genuinely taken aback.

"Oh dear!" he said. "Have I done something contrary to your Earth customs? On Yassacca it is traditional for the host to go through his guests' handbags and do little repairs and mending jobs on the contents . . ."

"Well . . . it's not an Earth custom . . ." said Nettie, still furious. "But . . . thanks for developing the film for me. That's exactly what I was looking for."

"It was my pleasure," said Corporal Golholiwol, gazing adoringly at Nettie. "Most of the photos seem to have come out OK. I also reelectroplated your nail scissors, restored several missing teeth to your comb, and resilvered your little mirror."

"Why! Thank you so much, Corporal!" Nettie had regained her composure and was searching through the photographs that Golholiwol had developed. Then suddenly she found what she was looking for. "Here! Look, Dan! It's the rectory! They came out! Those long exposures I took! THEY CAME OUT!"

Dan felt he was a bit out of his depth, but he just

said, without enthusiasm: "Oh, good! It'll be nice to have a souvenir."

Nettie, however, had already spun round and run off toward a group of Yassaccans who were talking gloomily over the roasting snork.

"Rodden!" Nettie called out, and the Navigational Officer turned around. "Rodden! I've got it! YOU CAN GET US BACK TO EARTH!" Nettie thrust two of the photographs into his hands. He took them unwillingly, not wishing to get involved in any fantasy that this alien female may have concocted.

"Well!" cried Nettie, hardly able to contain her excitement. "Look at them! What do you see?"

Rodden reluctantly looked down at the photos in his hand, and studied them. "It's a house . . . on Earth I assume . . ." he said slowly. "A former rectory . . . by the look of it . . . with planning permission for commercial use . . ."

"That's amazing!" exclaimed Nettie. "How d'you know all that?"

The Navigational Officer smiled smugly as he took off his translatorspecs and said: "It's written on the estate agents' board." He loved baffling beautiful but not too bright females.

"Oh! Right . . . Anyway, it's the place Dan and Lucy were going to buy before your Starship smashed into it."

"So?" Rodden was suddenly looking at them with increasing attention. "How do you suppose these will help you?"

"I took them at night!" cried Nettie excitedly. "Look at the sky! Especially that one, there! Look!"

A broad smile suddenly creased across Rodden's face.

"YOU CAN SEE THE STARS!" cried Nettie.

"My dear young woman," said Rodden. "You must forgive me for underestimating your . . ."

"Easy-over on the flattery!" replied Nettie. "I don't mind what you thought! The main thing is can you get any coordinates on those star patterns that will show where Earth is? Are there enough stars in the shot?"

Rodden was silent for some time. Nettie watched him anxiously, and suddenly Dan, who had just joined them, found Nettie's hand in his and she was squeezing it.

Rodden stared and stared at the photo. Finally he looked up. "Theoretically," he said. "It should be a simple question of three-dimensional geometry. There is only one place in the Galaxy in which the stars will appear in that exact configuration. . . . But I'm not sure this photo will provide enough information."

The Earth folks' hearts sank. The Navigational Officer was clearly trying to let them down gently. Nettie cursed herself; she had allowed her hopes to get too high. She was always doing that—especially with her men.

"But," the Navigational Officer was continuing, "I think I could enhance the image—do you have the negative?"

"It's here!" shouted Corporal Golholiwol.

"Then let's see what we can do," said Rodden. And with that the party suddenly started to seem more cheerful for everybody concerned.

24

It took two Dormillion days to run the enhanced photos of the night sky on Earth through the Great Astronomical Computer at the University of Yassaccanda. The computer went through fifteen trillion billion five hundred thousand million seven thousand four hundred and sixty-nine different comparisons before it finally came up with a star configuration that matched. It was on an outer spiral arm of the Galaxy in a sector that, quite frankly, had always been assumed to be uninhabitable.

"Alas!" said Rodden, the Navigational Officer, "it will take a long time to reach such a distant place!"

Nettie still had hold of Dan's hand. It seemed to Dan that she had permanently held on to his hand since that first discovery of the photos. Of course she hadn't, but it was just that Dan only counted himself alive at those moments when she had. But he daren't say anything more to her. He would never use her as "an emotional doormat"—she could be sure of that.

"We've only four more Dormillion days before the bomb goes off!" Nettie said. "How long will it take to get to Earth?"

Rodden paused before he spoke. He wanted to be exact. He didn't want to raise forlorn hopes in anyone—least of all himself. Finally he said: "To get to such a remote location would take three Dormillion weeks at best . . ."

Nettie leaned her head against Dan's shoulder and burst into tears. It was just too much. The thin edge of hope upon which she had been balancing for the last two days had suddenly given way. Dan put his arm around her and felt the softness of her shoulders.

"Nettie!" he said. "You'll be all right! You'll make a life here. Yassacca is beautiful!" As beautiful as you, he wanted to add, but thought better of it. Nettie, meanwhile, held on to Dan's arm as if it were her lifebelt.

"However," continued Rodden, "the *Starship Titanic* is propelled by a totally new and immeasurably more powerful drive. Judging by the time that elapsed since the launch, the crash on Earth, and the time when we picked you up, I would say the Starship must be capable of reaching the Earth in perhaps three Dormillion days."

Was it good news or bad news? Three Dormillion days! That would give them barely one day on Earth to find Leovinus and then, assuming he still had it in his possession, get the missing central intelligence core back into Titania's brain.

The only thing that was certain was that they must start now.

The first problem, however, was to find Lucy. After her last conversation with Dan, Lucy had been considering her life. She had slipped into a silky Yassaccan shift and gone for a long walk along the beach at Yassaccanda. The red waves, beating on the blue shore, made the same reassuring sounds that the waves made back home in Topanga. But somehow the comfort it brought her didn't make her long for home. Something had changed inside her. Something had died. Something had grown. Lucy was just trying to decide what it was when Nettie found her.

"Lucy! They've got the coordinates of Earth! We're going home! But we've got to hurry!" Nettie had never been one to beat about the bush. "By the way, you look great in that!"

"Thanks ... but ..." Lucy was gazing out across the unfamiliar seascape. "I'm going to stay here," she said.

"What on Earth are you talking about?" exclaimed Nettie. "We can go *home*!"

"I don't know where my home is anymore," said Lucy. "L.A.? London? Oxfordshire? I used to think it was anywhere Dan was, but now . . ."

"What's the matter between you and Dan?" Nettie was genuinely concerned for them, and had been ever since Dan's inexplicable behavior when she had been looking for her handbag.

"Neither of us wanted the rectory," Lucy turned and looked at Nettie for the first time.

"What?" exclaimed Nettie.

"It's as simple as that. We must have been fooling each other for years. . . . About all sorts of things . . . You know I was originally in love with Nigel?" Lucy was letting the sea wash around her bare feet.

"Till you realized what a shit he was?" asked Nettie.

"Not quite . . . It was more like . . . How can I describe it? Nigel was English . . . different . . . exciting. He made me feel all goose pimples inside. It was unsettling. . . . Whereas Dan I could understand. . . . Dan was familiar territory where I knew where I was."

"But Dan's gorgeous!" exclaimed Nettie. "He's so exciting! So different from the rest of them! From creeps like Nigel!" Lucy looked at Nettie in frank surprise. "I'm sorry!" Nettie continued. "I shouldn't talk about Dan like that. I didn't mean anything. . . . Anyway, we've got to hurry."

"Hurry away . . . run off . . . I've always done that, Nettie. I've wrapped my emotions up in a nice smart pin-striped suit and then walked away from them. Well, I'm not doing it any longer."

"But Dan needs you, Lucy! You're a great team!"

"That's what we kept telling each other. We told each other that over and over again until we believed it. But all I know is that I'm a different woman from the woman I've been pretending to be."

"Lucy!"

Lucy and Nettie spun round. They hadn't heard anyone approaching.

"Lucy! The Starship's about to take off for Earth!" It was The Journalist shouting from the breakwater. "We've only got a few minutes to make it!"

"We?" murmured Lucy.

"Of course!" exclaimed The Journalist. "You don't think I'd let you go back on your own. . . . Not now you've said you'll marry me!"

"But . . . The! I'll stay with you here if you want me to!" Lucy had run up to him and was kissing him.

"Uh-uh!" said The Journalist. "I've got to see this thing through to the end!"

And suddenly the three of them were racing along the sands toward the spaceport.

25

The journey back to Earth in the *Starship Titanic* was pretty uneventful for the first hundred and seventeen million million miles. The Deskbot was just as snooty as always, but since Lucy, Nettie, Dan, and The Journalist were traveling First Class (V.I.P. Status) all the other bots were unbelievably obsequious. The Liftbots gave Dan a surprising account of the Dunkirk evacuation which made it sound like a great victory for the Allied Forces, and the Deskbot asked for Nettie's autograph (nobody was quite sure why until they overheard the Deskbot whisper to one of

the Doorbots: "That's Gloria Stanley, the actress, you know!").
But otherwise routine life aboard the Starship ticked on.

Captain Bolfass put a brave face on his hopeless passion for
Nettie. And yet, as he told his wife, it had at least given some
purpose to his old age—even if that purpose were just to get
over it.

Nettie, for her part, was mainly concerned for Dan. He
seemed to be taking his separation from Lucy and her wild
affair with The Journalist rather badly. He mostly kept to his
cabin, and when he ate with them he was generally silent and
morose.

"Poor Dan!" Nettie thought to herself. "He must be going
through hell; after all, he and Lucy have been so close for all
those years, and now to see her so besotted with another
man—and an alien at that!"

Lucy and The Journalist also mostly kept to their cabin,
but judging from the sounds emanating from behind their
closed door, they were not brooding about anything. It
sounded as if they might have been playing polo, or doing a
bit of waterskiing all mixed in with some pretty serious
weight-lifting. All-in-all it was lucky the staterooms on either
side were empty. Even as it was, several pictures fell off the
adjoining walls and a stand bearing a pot of Yassaccan lilies
mysteriously toppled over.

On the third day the great Starship moved into the region of space beyond Proxima Centauri.

"We should locate your star any minute—what d'you call it?" asked Captain Bolfass.

"The Sun," said Nettie.

"What a beautiful name," said the gallant Captain, gazing at Nettie's exquisite profile.

Nettie nodded. "It's a beautiful thing."

"Hmmm," agreed the Captain dreamily.

"Do you recognize any of the star patterns yet?" asked the Navigational Officer anxiously. It was all very well heading for an unknown destination with such scanty data, but in this case they were all on board a ship that was destined to explode within two days' time! The whole venture was crazy as far as he was concerned, and he had expressed his opinion quite forcibly to Captain Bolfass. Supposing they failed to find Earth—would they ever find anywhere to land in this remote armpit of the Galaxy? And even if they did, once the Starship had exploded, they would be marooned for . . . well, goodness knows how long it would take a rescue fleet to arrive.

Nettie shook her head. "I'm not much good at astronomy! I'll get the others up on deck."

But neither Dan nor Lucy had any more idea than Nettie about the local constellations, and Rodden shook his head wearily at the Earth folk's ignorance.

"Perhaps you can't see the stars from the surface of your

planet?" he offered. But they had to admit they could, and felt twice as stupid.

But worse was to come.

"Look!" Rodden suddenly exclaimed. "D'you see that star! There! That must be your Sun!"

And so it proved to be. Within the hour the Starship was slowing down, and they could clearly see the Sun as a tiny disc.

"And so which of its planets is the Earth?" It was a simple question Rodden had asked, but it threw the three Earth folk into utter confusion.

"I *think* it's the fourth planet from the Sun," ventured Dan.

"Or is it the third?" asked Nettie.

"It's the second!" said Lucy.

The Navigational Officer had to excuse himself at this point. He left the Bridge and locked himself in the washroom, where he proceeded to bang his head against the sink unit for several minutes. How could any living creatures be so utterly and abysmally ignorant of their own planet?!

"Look!" said Dan. "On the outside: Pluto, right?"

"Yes."

"Neptune . . . Saturn . . . or is it Jupiter next?"

"Saturn," said Nettie.

"Saturn . . . Jupiter . . . Mars . . . Earth! So it's the sixth planet in!"

"Very good!" exclaimed Captain Bolfass. "Then we are

approaching it at this very moment! Stand by to fire retardation rockets and stabilize ship for slowdown! Orbit around Earth to be established in thirty-five edoes' time. Landing by small landing craft."

By the time the Navigational Officer came out of the washroom, the *Starship Titanic* was in orbit around Earth.

"Do the Starship windows make everything look red?" asked Nettie.

"Maybe it's the weather," said Lucy. The Earth did look extremely red.

"Ladies and gentlemen," said Captain Bolfass. "It is my privilege to accompany you down to your landing craft. If you would follow me . . ."

"Hang on!" said Nettie. "We forgot Uranus! This is Mars!"

The Navigational Officer left the room again. He could feel one of those terrible Yassaccan rages overtaking him. In the washroom, he got out his SD gun and blew his own head off. After which he calmed down and returned to the Bridge.

By this time, they were approaching a blue planet, patched with brown and flecked with white whorls. It was definitely Earth; even old Rodden couldn't help feeling sympathetically toward the three Earth folk as he saw their spirits rise and their hearts beat with pride and wonder at this vision of the planet that had given them life.

As they assembled in the tiny landing spacecraft, Bolfass spoke briefly and unemotionally.

"We have been assuming we have exactly one day in which to find Leovinus and, hopefully, the *Titanic's* missing central intelligence core, and get it back to the ship and into Titania's brain. But we have less than that. I did not mention this before, but I have to now. . . . We only have *half a day*, since, if you have not returned by midday, we will have no option but to fly the Starship off to a safe distance and man the lifeboats before she explodes. May we all be saved from such a fate. Go! And good luck!"

Nettie took Dan's hand as he helped her into the landing craft. The Journalist jumped in beside Lucy. "Oh, Dan?" he said. "There's something I've been meaning to ask you."

"Well, go ahead."

"Will you be our best man?"

Dan thought about hitting The Journalist but instead he smiled. "Yes," he replied. "I'll be glad to."

"Great!" smiled The Journalist. "We can have a real Blerontinian White Wedding. You'll love it."

Dan raised his eyes heavenwards and Nettie smiled, as the cover of the landing craft was placed over them.

Captain Bolfass retreated to the viewing chamber; the side of the great Starship opened, and the tiny landing craft blasted itself away toward the blue planet.

26

Leovinus was not in a good mood. Despite all the things he was good at—astrophysics, architecture, molecular biology, geophysics, painting, sculpture, mechanical design, physics, anatomy, music, poetry, crystallography, thermodynamics, electromagnetism, philosophy, and canapé arrangement—he'd always been hopeless at languages. Consequently, when he found himself on an alien world, without a translation blister, he was understandably frustrated. Here he was, the Greatest Genius the Galaxy Had Ever Known, and he couldn't even ask these aliens, in their strange blue suits, for a cup of tea.

"I definitely think he is, Sarge," said Constable Hackett.

"What, gay?" asked Sergeant Stroud, who'd noticed the old man's eyebrows were stuck on with toupee tape.

"No, Lebanese," said the Constable.

"Do we know anyone in the Oxford area who speaks Lebanese?"

"Well, it's kind of Arabic, innit?"

"Yes, must be plenty of them at the University," and so a call was made, and Leovinus shortly found himself confronted by a large man with a nose the shape of Africa who told him in Arabic that his name was Professor Dansak. But to no avail.

Leovinus was beginning to lose his temper by now. Not only was no one treating him as you would expect a race of clearly inferior minds to treat the Greatest Genius the Galaxy Has Ever Known, but everyone was treating him as if they actually wanted to get rid of him.

"I hereby charge you with being an illegal immigrant." Sergeant Stroud was reading from a formal charge-sheet. "I have to warn you that anything you may say will be held against you and that you will be held in a place of custody until such time as Her Majesty's Government is able to repatriate you to your own country."

"Assuming we can find out where that is," muttered Constable Hackett.

Professor Dansak had recommended a Professor

Lindstrom, who held the chair in Linguistic Studies. Professor Lindstrom listened carefully to the little that Leovinus was prepared to say to him, and concluded that the elderly gentleman in the white beard and false eyebrows was probably making the language up.

"It bears no resemblance to any of the Indo-European branch of languages," said Professor Lindstrom. "If indeed it *is* a language, I am prepared to state categorically that it has no relation to Uralic, Altaic, or to the Sino-Tibetan language groups. Malayo-Polynesian is not my field, but I would be surprised if it had any affinity there. As for the Eskimo-Aleut and the Paleo-Asiatic, I am convinced it is not. I suspect, in short, gentlemen, that you have here a confused old gentleman, talking that widely spoken language: gobbledygook. He probably ought to be with his family at home or else being cared for in an institution."

Leovinus at this point had decided to treat these inferior beings to a recitation of edited highlights from his recent work: *The Laws of Physics,* a radical reappraisal of the subject which had turned the entire science community on its head. It was, perhaps, the single most important volume ever written in the Galaxy, and merely to hear it again gave the great man a sense of belonging, and reminded him that he was an individual of immense importance—no matter how they treated him on this remote and primitive planet.

He was still reciting from his Tenth Law of Thermodynamic Stress when Sergeant Stroud banged the door of his cell behind him. Leovinus looked around his new environ-ment. His suspicion was that he was not in a hotel. Entry appeared to be regulated by a simple locking device, and defecation appeared to be in a bucket. What a savage world he had got himself stuck on.

If only he'd regained consciousness before the Starship crash-landed! But he hadn't. After his fight with Scraliontis, he'd remained unconscious throughout the entire launch, the SMEF (Spontaneous Massive Existence Failure), and the crash-landing on this godforsaken planet, wherever it was. He'd only come to when that wretched journalist had unrolled him from the curtain. Thinking it was still the morn-ing before the launch and that Scraliontis must have returned home to gloat over his evil scheme, Leovinus had comman-deered the service-lift and charged off out of the Starship screaming for revenge. In the dark he had failed to notice that he was no longer on the launchpad at Blerontis. It was not until he was a good distance from the ship that he heard the sound of the great power-drive coming to life. He had spun round and watched his great masterpiece rise up into an alien night sky. It was at that moment that he realized he was stranded on an unknown, unidentifiable world.

In a state of shock, Leovinus opened the door of a small vehicle he happened to find parked nearby, and climbed in. The vehicle was, as it turned out, already occupied by a par-ticularly dim-looking alien who nearly wet himself with ter-ror when confronted by Leovinus. The Great Man himself was, for the first time in his life, unable to think of anything to say—aware that whatever he *did* say would not be understandable. He had therefore sat there, without speaking, and allowed the alien to drive him to the present building in which he found himself and which he was increasingly convinced was *not* a hotel.

What a complete and absolute mess.

"FOR GOD'S SAKE! I WANT TO SEE A LAWYER!" Leovinus screamed at the top of his voice, and he rattled the bars of his cell in the time-honored tradition.

Sergeant Stroud looked at Constable Hackett and they both shook their heads. He might be a harmless, confused old man, but as far as they were concerned, it looked better in the station log if he were an illegal immigrant. They'd score a few points with the Home Office if they could get him sent back to somewhere or other . . . Maybe Chad or Zimbabwe . . .

27

•

Lucy thrilled to the expert way The Journalist brought the landing craft down in what had been the garden of the old rectory. In the darkness, the ruined house looked even more desolate than it had on that fateful night: souvenir hunters had stripped it of everything movable, including loose bricks.

The plan was to try and pick up Leovinus's trail, starting from the crash site. There was also the possibility that he might still be hanging around, hoping the Starship would return.

It was not a bad plan, as such, but as Dan

jumped out of the landing craft a loudspeaker crackled across the old rectory lawns and a blinding searchlight hit him full in the face: "Put your hands above your heads! Do not make any sudden movements! You are surrounded by armed police!" They had not reckoned on the Oxfordshire Constabulary, who, flushed with their recent success in capturing an illegal immigrant, had set up a permanent watch around the landing site.

Dan instinctively did all the things the megaphone had told him not to do. He didn't put his hands above his head. He leapt—very suddenly—back into the landing craft and screamed: "Hit it!"

The Journalist fired the engine and the small craft leapt into the air, as a hail of gunfire exploded across the lawn. In a few seconds, the spacecraft had disappeared into the night, and the Oxfordshire Police were left staring at the empty sward.

"Calm down, everyone!" Nettie had taken over, although Lucy was contributing the most volubly to the discussion:

"Aaaarrrgh! Agggh!" She was choosing her words carefully.

The Journalist was concentrating on controlling the craft. Dan was shaking.

"OK," continued Nettie. "We've got twelve hours to find Leovinus. Our two chances are: one, picking up his trail around here, and two, Nigel."

"Nigel?" Dan's hackles were up—could this wonderful woman still be thinking about that schmuck?

"He's the one person we know was here at the site when Leovinus walked off the ship. He may have seen him—may even know where he is now!"

"Nettie! You're a genius!" said Dan.

"Aaaah! Ooooh!" Lucy added.

"I suggest you and Lucy investigate around here, while The, here, drives me to London to find Nigel." Nettie had it all worked out. Within a few minutes, the landing craft had deposited Dan and Lucy in a quiet back lane near the hotel where they had been staying, and in another minute, Nettie and The Journalist were heading for the M40.

It began to get light as they approached the motorway. "We don't want the police picking us up," Nettie was thinking aloud. "We'd better pretend we're an ordinary car—a Japanese copy of something Italian maybe. Can you drive this thing just a few inches above the ground?"

"Absolutely!" said The Journalist, and he swung the craft down onto the empty B road. It took him a few moments to pick up the knack of keeping it steady at such a low altitude, but he was getting it.

"And you'd better cut the speed down just a tad, The," said Nettie. "One hundred eighty miles an hour is a little fast for these bends."

By the time they swung out into the fast lane of the M40, The Journalist had managed to get the craft down to a mere 80 mph and was giving a pretty good impression of a perfectly ordinary (if flamboyantly designed) motorcar. Nettie just hoped nobody would notice their lack of wheels.

Being the rush hour, most drivers weren't looking where they were going, as they crawled their way toward Central London. The finest jam, however, was reserved for the picturesque stretch after the Uxbridge turnoff. There was road construction, and the rush hour simply ground to a deadening halt.

"Purple Pangalin!" exclaimed The Journalist. "What sort of a transportation system d'you call this? The more popular it is the slower it goes! What genius worked this out?!" He was really quite indignant.

"Well, it's inevitable isn't it?" Nettie found herself being surprisingly defensive of her planet's right to have traffic jams.

"Of course it isn't!" exploded The Journalist. "You have to devise a system that goes *faster* the more popular it is, so it can cope! It's perfectly obvious!"

Nettie was drumming her fingers on the dashboard of the landing craft, and smiling at anyone who happened to give them an odd look. Smiling was always the best way to make them look away. She was also glancing with increasing frequency at her watch. Time was running out.

The jam moved an inch nearer London.

"I mean a transportation system with an average speed of just above stationary is not really a transportation system at all!" The Journalist was raving by now. "It's more like a storage system!"

"OK! Let's do it!" Nettie suddenly sounded decisive. "I've always fantasized about this!"

"What?"

"Take her up! Nobody's watching!"

And sure enough, when The Journalist gunned the spacecraft up into the air and sped over the heads of the preceding traffic, nobody seemed to notice. He set the craft down again in an open space on the other side of the jam. The driver of the car they landed in front of was not a happily married man. He had been mulling over what would happen if his wife never returned from the skiing holiday she was currently enjoying. Perhaps she would run off with the instructor and breed Alpine sheep and serve English teas to walkers in the summer. But then there were the children. He'd have to get them to school every day on his own and he wouldn't be able to stay at the office after hours to chat up that new secretary. . . . At this moment a sporty-looking car suddenly appeared in front of him. "Jesus!" he exclaimed, swerving involuntarily, "I didn't even notice it overtaking! God! The speed some people drive at!"

It was only as the sporty car sped away in the fast lane that he noticed it didn't seem to have any wheels. "Concentrate!" he told himself. "Otherwise you start seeing things."

Another jam brought them to a resounding halt just as they reached the Westway overpass.

"Oh no!" groaned Nettie.

"We used to have problems like this on Blerontin," observed The Journalist. "Several million years ago, before intelligent life developed."

"Oh shut up!" said Nettie. She couldn't bear self-satisfied aliens who couldn't see any of the good things about Earth. "This is hopeless. We've only got nine hours left!"

"Where have we got to get to?"

"The Earls Court Road," Nettie replied.

"Shall we take the short cut?"

Nettie looked around. There were no police cars as far as she could see, and the woman in the car behind was picking her fingernails.

"Go for it!" she said, and the craft left the overpass to the amazement of a couple of small children who were on their way to school.

"Look, Mum! That car's flying!"

"Well I never, dear," said their mother, without taking her eyes off the *Hello* magazine she was reading. "Whatever will we see next!"

Nettie and The Journalist swooped low over Notting Hill and effected a landing on the south side of Holland Park. Here they waited their moment, hopped over a closed gate, and filtered into the one-way system around Earl's Court.

"Eight-thirty!" said Nettie, leaping out of the "car." "You stay here! If I know that sleazeball Nigel, he'll still be in bed!"

She used her key to get in, and was soon racing up

the stairs to Nigel's flat. She let herself in and immediately fell over a broken ironing board that was lying across the doorway.

"Who's that?" called a voice from the bedroom.

"It's me!" yelled Nettie, picking herself up and striding into the bedroom.

The young girl with whom Nigel was currently engaged tried to pretend she was merely sitting astride a pile of old laundry.

"Shit! Nettie!" exclaimed Nigel, making an effort to disguise himself as the pile of old laundry in question by pulling all the sheets around himself. "I thought you'd been abducted by aliens!"

"This is important, Nigel!" Nettie was straight to the point.

"I can explain all this . . ." Nigel began. "You see, this is Nancy, and her mother died recently and I've been looking after . . ."

"Think back, Nigel! After the spaceship took off, did you see anyone?"

"You mean like going to a psychiatrist?"

"No! No!" Trust Nigel to be only thinking of himself, thought Nettie. "Did you see an old man with a white beard, hanging around the wreckage?"

"I think I'd better go," said Nancy, who was actually nineteen but looked younger.

"No! No! Hang on," said Nigel instinctively. He could see that Nettie had other things on her mind than putting his balls in the toaster, and he half hoped he might be able to resume what he had been doing, once he'd sorted out whatever it was his ex-girlfriend actually *did* want of him. "Did I see *what*?"

Nettie was suddenly overwhelmed by the hopelessness of it all. Here was a whole world—a whole civilization so much more advanced than her own—depending on her eliciting a sensible answer from this creep whom she'd once been in love with. What a hope in hell! She might as well try and teach Turkish to the cat!

"An old man with a white beard?" said Nigel. "He was in my car. I took him to Oxford police station."

It took Nettie a moment to realize that this was exactly the information she had come all this way to extract. The moment she did, Nettie ran to the bed and gave Nigel a smacking kiss on the lips. Then she gave one to Nancy for good measure, and the next minute she was leaping down the stone stairs of the large Victorian mansion two at a time, whooping: "The! The! The!"

"I think I'd better go," said Nancy. She was just about to start a degree in Art History.

28

●

Leovinus had undergone a sea change.

For a start, he had taken off his false eye-brows and stuck them on the wall of his cell, just above the door. But even more importantly, he had spent the last week doing something that he had never really done before—certainly not since the early days when he was on the verge of becoming an infant prodigy. Seven days in a prison cell, without reading materials, without any ability to communicate with others, and, what's more, without a single admirer, had forced him to take stock of himself. He had spent a week looking back at his life and at the person he had become. And the more he had done this, the more he had become convinced that he had failed. The more he looked into his own soul, the more he realized how far short he fell.

He flinched with acute embarrassment as he remembered that last press conference—how he had reveled in the sycophancy. He curled up with shame as he remembered the answer he had given to that journalist who had asked if he felt responsible for the collapse of the Yassaccan economy. What had he said? "His responsibility was toward his Art" or something like that? Now, as he stared round at the bare walls of his cell, he realized that he'd been talking through his bottom. No one could hide behind the pretensions of creativity when people were actually suffering—maybe even dying—because of it.

He remembered the two cub reporters with their lovely smiles and alluring green lipstick . . . How he had felt so superior to them . . . How he'd believed deep down that no one was good enough for him. Now, the more he looked about himself, in the solitude and misery of his prison cell, the more he felt *he* was not good enough for anyone *else*. The first Blerontinian who walked in through that door, he began to think, would have more right to freedom and happiness than he had. Even that dreadful Gat of Blerontis!

Leovinus had been granted such wonderful gifts—such fabulous, unlimited gifts—and what had he done with them?

Had he made anyone else happy? Had he brought prosperity and peace to other worlds? No. As far as Leovinus could see, he had used his gifts almost exclusively for his own self-aggrandizement. Full stop. It was pathetic, now that he looked back. Had he been loved? Had he loved?

And here, had you been eavesdropping outside the great man's cell (as indeed Constable Hackett was doing) then you would have heard a terrible groan rise up from the Greatest Genius the Galaxy Had Ever Known, as he remembered how his love and affection had been focused not on a living creature—not on a wife, not on a lover, not even on a pet snorkling!—but on an agglomeration of wires and neurons, sensors and cybernetic pathways—Titania—his last, his greatest, his absolute obsession!

"But she loves me!" he cried from the depths of his despair.

"But she is not real . . ." came an answering echo as his thoughts bounced off the bare cell walls. "You created her!"

This change that overcame Leovinus, in his Oxfordshire prison cell, would be unfortunately powerful ammunition for right-wing politicians who trumpet the beneficial effects of jail. Fortunately, however, it went totally unnoticed by anyone with political clout on Earth.

Leovinus had just reached that point of self-castigation at which he was really beginning to enjoy it when he was rudely interrupted.

"Visitors for you, Chang!" said Constable Hackett. He had grown rather fond of the old fellow over the past week.

The door was flung open and the dreadful journalist entered accompanied by an extraordinarily attractive female alien, all the more attractive for being dressed Yassaccan style, in the simple shift with the single motif on the side which indicated that the wearer was unmarried and interested in marriage proposals.

She was also wearing that fabulously expensive Yassaccan scent that was now almost unobtainable on Blerontin.

"My dear friend!" exclaimed Leovinus to The (surprised) Journalist. "You are far more worthy of freedom and happiness than I!" It was an odd thing to say to the first Blerontinian to walk in through the door, but Leovinus, who had just been thinking he'd never get a chance to say it, said it anyway.

"There's not a moment to lose!" exclaimed the remarkably attractive and remarkably available female alien. "We've only got an hour left!"

"Have you got it?" cried The Journalist.

"I don't know . . ." replied Leovinus. "I am no longer sure what I have got and what I have not. When I look back on my life, I almost feel I have thrown it all away and I have been left with nothing. Dear lady, will you marry me?"

Leovinus knew it was considered poor manners not to propose to any young female wearing the specially patterned shift.

"Have you got the central intelligence core? Titania's brain!" interposed The Journalist before Nettie could reply.

"Ah! Alas!" cried the great Leovinus. "I threw it away! I have no use for her now!" and he turned back to Nettie. "Dear lady! Do you think you could ever love me?"

"YOU CAN'T HAVE THROWN IT AWAY!" screamed the remarkably attractive and available female alien.

"THINK!" yelled the dreadful journalist. "Where did you throw it?"

"What does it matter?" Leovinus had grown a trifle maudlin. This was actually the result of the famous Yassaccan scent which the Yassaccan Prime Minister had given Nettie, and which she was now wearing for the first time. Nettie had dabbed a spot on as they waited for the cell door to be opened—it was a nervous reflex prior to meeting the Greatest Genius the Galaxy Had Ever Known. What Nettie was unaware of was that one of the reasons the Yassaccan scent was so famous was because it had an extremely intoxicating effect on Blerontinians. This intoxication was usually so sudden and so strong that the scent had been made illegal on Blerontin, which is, of course, why it was so sought after and so fabulously expensive.

"My dear lady! My life! How I have longed to meet someone as beautiful and intelligent as you!"

The Journalist had now grabbed Leovinus by the lapels

of his prison suit. "WHERE IS TITANIA'S BRAIN?" he yelled.

Leovinus was rapidly deteriorating under the powerful influence of Nettie's scent. "Ha! Mr. Journalisto! See one oh dee crank? Pon flee up and trick?" Leovinus was quoting a Blerontinian nonsense rhyme that was often sung to children at bedtime.

"Salk tense, man!" shouted The Journalist, who had suddenly realized what kind of scent Nettie was wearing. "'Svital we know where youze threw th'central telligence core—*hic*!" Oh no! If he got drunk he wouldn't be able to drive them back to the Starship!

"Nettie!" he screamed. "Quick! Youze gotter grout of here!"

"Not on your life!" exclaimed Nettie. "You think you can handle this better just cause you're a man?"

"No . . . no . . . I'm not a man. . . . That is . . . I'm a Blerontinian. . . ." The Journalist had started giggling. Now Leovinus started, too.

"Stop it!" cried Nettie, trying to shake some sense into them. "How can you laugh? We've got to find Titania's intelligence core! Where is it, Leovinus?" But the more she shook them, the more the Yassaccan scent wafted up from her beautiful body and blew the minds of the two Blerontinians . . . and they laughed harder and harder until tears were rolling down their cheeks. Leovinus found his head spinning. The Journalist started to sing an old Blerontinian song about a lady acrobat and a news reporter, and then collapsed on the bed.

Finally Nettie gave up in disgust. She stormed out of the cell to find the Desk Sergeant. Perhaps he had Titania's missing piece in safe custody.

The moment Nettie had gone, The Journalist made a valiant attempt to pull himself together. He managed to stop laughing, with partial success, and, as his head began to clear, he turned on Leovinus and shook him, until the old man regained his senses.

"THINK!" cried The Journalist. "Even if you've never done anything decent in the whole of your wretched life! Do it now! Remember where you threw the missing bit of Titania's brain?"

This appeal could not have been more calculated to penetrate through to Leovinus's great, though intoxicated, brain. "The central intelligence core ... Titania's cerebral artery ... Where did I throw it?"

"Yes! Dammit, man! Where did you throw it?"

"Oh! I know! In the corner ... over there...." The Great Man pointed to a corner of the cell. In a flash, The Journalist was there, scrabbling around behind the latrine bucket, and the next moment he suddenly stood up with a glowing silver shard in his hand.

But before he even had time to give a yell of triumph, Nettie appeared at the cell door. "We're too late!" she announced. "My watch must have been wrong. According to the police station clock, it's already midday. . . ." And even as she spoke, they heard the BBC's pips from the Superintendent's radio. The *Starship Titanic* would already be on its way to its graveyard in space.

29

Dan and Lucy had had a miserable time of it. They had traipsed around the Oxfordshire countryside with a growing feeling of helplessness. Nobody had seen any old man with a white beard. Nobody had heard of aliens arriving from outer space. Nobody wanted to know either. Such things didn't happen in Oxfordshire.

Finally they retraced their steps to the hotel where they had all been staying. Here again they had drawn a blank. Yes, Nigel had checked out that day. No, he had not had anybody with him. No. No old man with a white beard had checked in. Nothing. Zero.

They sat over a miserable cup of coffee and Dan looked blankly at Lucy. She suddenly seemed so far away from him. Wasn't that what she had always said about him? That he had seemed so far away? He tried to think of all the things that had made them feel close in the past . . . and yet everything he thought of now appeared like a figment of his imagination. Like Lucy's enthusiasm for turning the old rectory into a hotel . . . In a way, he thought, their whole relationship had probably come out of his imagination. He had dreamed the whole thing up and now it was shattered, nothing remained between them. Not even bitterness.

Lucy watched Dan brooding over his coffee and wondered if he would be all right. She felt guilty. She felt she'd let him down. But now that she had discovered that there was a part of her that had been asleep, all the time she had been with Dan, she knew there was no turning back the clock. It was as if she herself had created the bond between them—a bond that protected her from other, stronger, more frightening feelings that she was capable of—but a bond that did not otherwise exist.

Lucy put her hand on Dan's. "I'm sorry," she said. To her surprise, Dan looked up and smiled. "We've been a good team," he said. "We've helped each other to get to where we are, and now I guess we're ready to move right on."

Lucy leaned across and kissed him lightly, and at that

very moment, Nettie, The Journalist, and Leovinus walked in the door.

By the time they had persuaded the Oxford constabulary that Leovinus was not an illegal immigrant (even though, technically speaking, he was) it was well after half-past one o'clock. By the time Nettie had been able to shower off all the intoxicating Yassaccan perfume, it was half-past two. And by the time they found Lucy and Dan, the deadline was well past. They all slumped in front of their coffees and nobody said a word, until Nettie suddenly looked up.

"Listen!" said Nettie. "It's no good us all just sitting here like burnt toast. I know there's not much point, but I suggest we go back to where we left the Starship in orbit—just in case—they may have left something—or somebody may have got left behind—or ... I don't know what. All I know is I won't be happy until I've seen it's not there."

"You are so charming, dear lady," said Leovinus, "and possess such a fine mind." It would be hard to say who was more jealous—Lucy or Dan. Neither of them said a word whatever and there followed a short argument about the futileness of doing what Nettie had suggested, which seemed about to segue into a discussion about the futility of existence itself, until Nettie cut it short. "Well, I'm going, will you take me, The?"

Strangely enough they all felt more cheerful as they took off in the tiny landing craft. The illusion of doing something, no matter how useless, is always good for the psyche. They roared up into the stratosphere and there, with Earth rolling beneath them—a wonderful ball of real life—they suddenly saw another, even more wonderful sight. An astonishing sight. A sight that made them cheer and shout and kiss each other. . . . And Dan found himself kissing Nettie and being kissed back by Nettie and then kissing Nettie again and then she was kissing old Leovinus and Dan reminded himself that she had rejected him before and there was no point in being hurt again. . . . And then he suddenly remembered the sight— the wonderful sight that had made them all cheer and start kissing each other in the first place: over the Earth's glowing blue and white shoulder heaved the immense and fabulous shape of the *Starship Titanic*!

"Of course!" yelled Nettie. "We're idiots! Captain Bolfass was talking about Dormillion days!" She checked her watch. "We've still got twenty minutes to go!"

Leovinus gazed into her beautiful face. Her eyelids fluttered, and slowly she opened her lovely eyes and gazed back at him. He had slipped the missing cerebral artery—the central intelligence core—into Titania's brain as gently as he could. He knew the shudder of life that would run through her would bring both joy and pain, as unused neurons and dormant cybernetic pathways pulsed into new life.

"Titania!" whispered the old man. "I still love you."

Nettie, Dan, and the others gasped as the beautiful creature raised her head off the floor, leaned up on one elbow, and then—her hair spilling around her shoulders—rose majestically, powerfully, and sat as she had always been designed to sit, with her chin resting thoughtfully upon her hand. Titania had come to life and the *Starship Titanic* was finally complete.

At once Nettie felt a change in the Starship—as if a powerful and benign presence were watching over them all—a presence that was hugely intelligent, kind, wise, caring, serene, warm . . . Nettie squeezed Dan's hand.

"Dan," she said, "would you kiss me again?"

And that, really, is the end of the story. Captain Bolfass, Lucy, and The Journalist were able to disarm the bomb as soon as Titania came to life—much to the bomb's relief; it had never really wanted to explode.

The grateful Yassaccans offered Dan, Nettie, Lucy, and The Journalist shares in the Starship as a reward for their part in saving it. They also invited Lucy and Dan to run it as a hotel.

Dan bowed out gracefully; he wanted to stay on Earth, he said, and so Lucy and The Journalist became the proprietors of Starship Titanic Hotel, Inc., the most hugely successful luxury holiday enterprise in the entire Galaxy—and one which put the Yassaccan economy back on its feet within the first year of operation.

The Yassaccans returned to their peaceful, prosperous way of life and craftsmanship, and celebrated the Starship with a full-scale statue (in superb detail—inside and out) in the main square of Yassaccanda.

Lucy and The Journalist were married, with elaborate ceremonies both here on Earth and on Blerontin. He wrote up his story and it became the scoop of the century, and made him so much money that he was able to give up journalism entirely and devote himself to more useful things. Being no longer a journalist, of course, also meant that he was able to tell Lucy his true name, which turned out to be: Tiddelpuss. So she called him Tiddles and that suited Lucy just fine. But he would never ever tell her what "Lucy" meant in Blerontinian.

Leovinus got over his momentary passion for Nettie, which had been partly brought on by the intoxicating effects of her perfume. He spent an increasing amount of time chatting to Titania in her private chamber. He knew she wasn't real, but then he had begun to think that perhaps he was too old for reality anyway. The Greatest Genius the Galaxy Has Ever Known regained a certain amount of his old self-confidence, but friends and admirers found him humbler and more sensitive to the needs of others. Perhaps it was Titania's influence. Perhaps it was the fact that his eyebrows had finally grown back.

The good Captain Bolfass, on the other hand, never really got over his infatuation for Nettie, although his wife bought him countless herbal remedies and embrocations. But the thought of Nettie kept him going in the dark watches of space, and enriched his declining years with a golden glow of tragic devotion. In fact, there were a great many Yassaccans who felt the same way about Nettie. The Yassaccans, you see, were the sort of people who could recognize a hugely intelligent, kind, wise, caring, serene, and warm being when they met one for real.

Nettie herself couldn't believe her luck when Lucy went off and married The Journalist. She immediately felt free to propose to Dan, and he couldn't believe his luck either. The two of them became not only lovers but best friends. Nettie took a degree in Higher Mathematics, and was able to help Old Leovinus on some of his later works. She made so much money out of this that she and Dan were able to rebuild the old rectory and turn it into a relaxed family hotel specializing in Central Galactic cuisine. In the entrance hall, visiting Yassaccan parents would point out to their children the famous framed photograph which bore the inscription: "Dan and Nettie's Hotel Beneath the Stars."

And the parrot? The parrot probably came out best of all—in parrot terms. It had, in fact, been acting as an undercover agent for the Yassaccans all along. It had been smuggled on board the *Starship Titanic* before the removal to Blerontin. The parrot had performed heroically, risking life and feathers, to get reports of the scandalously shoddy construction of the Starship back to Yassacca. It had, in fact, been the source of all the rumors that had been circulating. When the parrot eventually returned to its hometown on Yassacca, it was given a special golden perch and a medal, specially created for it, as the first parrot on Yassacca to be decorated for bravery and service to the planet.

It was also given a lifetime supply of millet seed and pistachio. It mated shortly after and became the proud mother of four baby parrots whom it named, Dan, Nettie, Lucy, and The.

Starship Titanic is also a unique adventure game, featuring cinematic quality graphics. The game employs a dynamic language processor which facilitates complex and entertaining conversations between you, the player, and the game's cast of colorful characters.

Available on CD-ROM for Windows 95 and Macintosh operating systems, *Douglas Adams's Starship Titanic* is published by Simon & Schuster Interactive and The Digital Village. You'll find copies at your favorite software retailer. For further information about the game visit the official Web site at:
http://www.starshiptitanic.com

To purchase a copy visit the Simon & Schuster Interactive Web site at:
http://www.ssinteractive.com

More news and info about Douglas Adams's new company, The Digital Village, and about the man himself at:
http://www.tdv.com

If you are interested in the works of Douglas Adams, you may like to join ZZ9 Plural Z Alpha, the official Hitchhiker's Guide to the Galaxy Appreciation Society. For details of this fan-run society, established for seventeen years, send a SAE/IRC to: 67 South Park Gardens, Berkhamsted, Herts HP4 1HZ, U.K. Or visit the ZZ9 Plural Z Alpha Web site at:
http://www.atomiser.demon.co.uk

Terry Jones fans, Monty Python fans, and Norwegians should visit:
http://www.pythonline.com